MURDER

UNDER THE LOON

OTHER BOOKS BY GERALD ANDERSON

Death Before Dinner
Midnight Ink, 2007

The Uffda Trial
Martin House, 1994

FORTHCOMING BY GERALD ANDERSON

Murder Under the Prairie Chicken

An Otter Tail County Mystery

MURDER
UNDER THE LOON

Gerald Anderson

MIDNIGHT INK
WOODBURY, MINNESOTA

First Edition
First Printing, 2008

Book design and format by Donna Burch
Cover design by Gavin Dayton Duffy
Cover art © 2007 Ron Chapple / JupiterImages Corporation / PunchStock
Midnight Ink, an imprint of Llewellyn Publications

Library of Congress Cataloging-in-Publication Data
Anderson, Gerald D., 1944–
    Murder under the loon : an Otter Tail County mystery / Gerald Anderson.
    — 1st ed.
            p.   cm.
    ISBN: 978-0-7387-1095-2
    1. Insurance executives—Crimes against—Fiction.   2. Executive succession—Fiction.   3. Winter resorts—Fiction.   4. Minnesota—Fiction.   I. Title.
    PS3601.N5436M87   2008
    813'.6—dc22   2007042481

Midnight Ink
Llewellyn Publications
2143 Wooddale Drive, Dept. 978-0-7387-1095-2
Woodbury, MN 55125-2989 USA
www.midnightinkbooks.com

Printed in the United States of America

*To Carmen N. Anderson, Karl A. Anderson,
and Paul M. Anderson—three remarkably intelligent,
sensitive, kind, and responsible citizens
of whom I am very proud*

PROLOGUE

It was twenty-one degrees below zero. A quarter-moon hung in the southern sky, but did not cast sufficient light to dull the effects of the aurora borealis in the northern sky. The northern lights shimmered and danced, first forming a curtain, then a halo, then a dazzling curtain again. The lights were green, then they were blue, then they were a greenish blue. On some nights, they acquired a certain pinkish hue, but not tonight, which was just as well, for there were few eyes turned to the heavens.

The only other light that quivered across the clear ice of a Minnesota lake, and the only sound that disturbed the total silence of the night came from the same source. It was a snowmobile, emitting a steady whine as it served an appointment with death. On this noisy motorized sled, a rider thought momentarily, "I love to ride my snowmobile; this is one of the most pleasant dreams I've ever had. But the sound is different from my own sled—maybe if I think real hard I can tell the model. But, ooooh, it hurts to think, and I'm so tired." And he stopped dreaming for a while.

Eventually, the snowmobile came to the edge of the lake and went up onto a bank that was covered in pure, white snow. The rider felt a tremendous thump on the top of his helmet, and it seemed as though the soft snow rose up to welcome him into fluffy, downy arms. An hour passed, during which he approached the edge of consciousness only to hear the drone of a snowmobile engine.

Then, with a sudden shock, his mind came back from black oblivion into a state of semi-consciousness. His brain was a collage of confusing sensations. "My God, our help in ages past!" he thought. "My head hurts something fierce. I can't bear to move it." It was only then that he became aware of the intense cold that actually hurt his teeth as he breathed in the night air. He could still hear the roar of a small engine and thought, "There's a snowmobile in my bedroom!" Then, "No, that must be coming from a snowmobile outside, but if that is so…?" For several minutes he lay motionless, listening to the machine and trying to will himself into consciousness. Finally, with tremendous effort, he opened his eyes. Without the strength to scream, he gazed in horror as he saw, illuminated by a billion stars floating in a black sky, a twenty-foot loon staring down at him.

ONE

JOHN HOFSTEAD WAS A pink man. His face had a uniform pinkness that extended from his closely shaved chin to his round, pink nose to his glowing pink, hairless scalp. The vast expanse of pink was interrupted only by two drifts of snow-white hair above his light blue eyes. The only other feature that relieved this ocean of pinkness was a uniform and carefully trimmed fringe of feathery white hair that created a shimmering curtain between the pink pate and the pink neck. From the rear, Hofstead's head looked like a maraschino cherry comfortably nestling in a mound of whipped cream. The overall effect of his pinkness extended even to his hands. The nails, clean and clipped short, had such a translucent quality that the slightly whiter cuticles served to define what looked like ten little buttons.

Perhaps it was something about this color, perhaps it was only the inner peace of the man showing through, but, in any event, Hofstead gave off the aura of a man at peace with himself and at peace with the world. He always wore a suit and tie, and in the winter he usually wore a vest as well. It was hard for anyone to see such a well-scrubbed man and not form an instant liking for him. His pale eyes were the epitome of openness, and it seemed impossible that they could hide any deceit. His soft laugh, which verged on a giggle, was disarming to the most hostile of potential foes. Somehow, and without contrivance, he even managed to smell clean. There was no odor of French cologne about him, just the consistent perfume of Ivory soap.

This was of great benefit to Hofstead in his chosen position. Hofstead was an insurance man. His ingenuous likability proved to be such a tremendous asset for sales that he founded, at the age of twenty-seven, his own insurance company. That was four decades ago, and Hofstead Hail Insurance was now one of the most prosperous firms in Fergus Falls, Minnesota. Hofstead Hail was successful, in part, because the owner and president genuinely believed in his product. He took pride in the fact that he refused to sell more insurance to a client than he really needed, and claimed that he got a great deal of personal satisfaction in handing over a claims check to a deserving farmer who had had the foresight to insure his crops with Hofstead Hail. To be sure, there were those who might have pointed out that Hofstead's idea of what people really needed in the way of insurance was somewhat grander than commonly accepted levels, but nobody could accuse him of not practicing what he preached. His car, his boat, his house, his business, and his teeth were all insured against any untoward event. His life was insured with policies that benefited his three loves. His wife, Martha, would be taken care of at the time of his being "called home," but so would his alma mater, Concordia College, the Lutheran college in Moorhead, Minnesota, to which he attributed every good thing that had happened in his life. His third and most recent love, and the beneficiary of his third major life insurance policy, was the student scholarship program, the "Hofstead Award," at the local Fergus Falls State University. The late president of FFSU, George Gherkin, had been extremely persuasive and, when he made the continuation of the college insurance contract contingent upon a meaningful contribution, Hofstead agreed to set up a scholarship fund that would be presented to graduates of Fergus Falls High School, the home of the Otters. He and Martha had never had children, and the intellectual progress of the Hofstead Scholars gave them special enjoyment.

It was a life that reflected accomplishment and personal fulfillment, and this was perhaps part of the reason that the giggles could gush forth so easily from his short and portly body. But it had also been a life of hard work, and the death of a close friend, the unfortunate George Gherkin, had brought home to Hofstead the fleeting nature of life on earth. Hofstead was now sixty-eight years old, and although he didn't really need it, he figured he should be collecting social security. It was time to stop and smell the roses, time to retire and spend all his days at the lake cottage, and time to go back to the old country and see where the Hofsteads had come from in Norway. And it was also time to spend the winters in Fort Meyers, Florida, and then watch the Minnesota Twins during spring training.

"The last winter in Minnesota," mused John Hofstead, as he gazed out the frosted windows of his office in the old Hotel Kaddatz. "Boy–oh-boy-oh-boy! I don't think I'm going to miss it at all. I'm going to give up ice fishing and snowmobiling for golfing in January. What a trade! What a glorious trade!" A smile of anticipation added dental whiteness to the expanses of pink. "And tonight, when I tell Martha the news, I'm going to start by telling her that I don't think she should go out and buy a new coat. Hee-hee. She'll say, 'But I need to replace my old one.' And then I'll say, 'No you don't! No you don't!' Hee-hee." He proceeded to write "Florida" in the frosty rime and with a warm pudgy finger melted the ice to form the dot over the i. He caught a reflection of his face in an unfrosted part of the window. "I'm going to spend my time in the sun and get a nice, deep tan," he promised himself.

Still, he knew he would miss his office in the old hotel. It was once the grandest hotel in western Minnesota, but when the interstate highway was built, newer hotels with swimming pools and plenty of parking spaces had been built on the edge of town. Only the locals, it seemed, came to downtown Fergus Falls anymore, and they usually didn't need a place to stay. For years the building stood empty, suffering the indignities of abandonment, the ravages of a leaking roof, expanding ice, pigeons, bats, and assorted vermin. Everyone in town wistfully waited for some white knight to open up the grand hotel once more. Finally, and inevitably, it appeared that it would have to be torn down. But John Hofstead, who had spent his wedding night with Martha in room 306, could not bear to see it go. He took the lead in investigating historic preservation grants. He persuaded a local architectural firm to examine the building and prepare projections for alternative uses. Finally, it was he who made the first commitment to relocate his business there. It had taken a lot of volunteer work for the painstaking restoration, and the top floor was still a long way from completion. The heating was inefficient and the windows would all have to be replaced eventually, but it was Hofstead's pride and joy, and when he overheard younger people refer to it as the "Hofstead building" he did not bother to correct them.

Hofstead Hail held a perpetual lease on the front half of the third floor, and it was no coincidence that his own office had once been Room 306. All of the other employees of Hofstead Hail, with the exception of seasonal adjusters (usually high school teachers who could not get a summer job as a driver's education instructor) were located in adjoining rooms. His faithful secretary, Mrs. Borghild Kvamme, could be found in an open area that had once been Room 302. Clarence Sandberg was in old Room 304, Gary Swenson was in Room 305, and Myron Pekanen was in Room 303. That left Room 301 vacant for Hofstead's special professional indulgence, an infrequently used conference room containing a large banquet table from the hotel's Western Empire Room.

The first thing Hofstead did when he decided to retire was to call a company meeting. It was a mark of his dedication to the firm that his employees would know about his plans even before his beloved Martha. He approached the meeting with undisguised glee, keeping all details secret from even the ever-curious Borghild. He wanted everything to be just right for this little swan song and, to his secretary's amazement, he was observed personally cleaning up the conference room, misting the surface of the large table with a can of Pledge. Carefully, the dapper pink man aligned chairs before the ubiquitous note pads and pencils, both of which were embossed with "Season's Greetings from Hofstead Hail." He even considered brewing a fresh pot of coffee for the meeting, but decided that Borghild could just as well maintain her most important office function.

His preparations complete, Hofstead instructed Mrs. Kvamme to hold all calls and proceeded to hole up in his office with the door closed, an occurrence remarkable in itself. For the next half hour, while Borghild used every last bit of her will power to avoid picking up the phone and listening, he was speaking on the telephone in a muffled voice.

At three o'clock, the permanent employees of the company found their way to the meeting room to take their positions at the table. They assumed, correctly, that the chair at the head of the table was reserved for the owner and president of Hofstead Hail. They also assumed that the chair immediately to the right was reserved for Mrs. Kvamme. What occurred next, however, could be seen as a portent of the struggle to come. Sandberg and Swenson entered the room at exactly the same time, a good ten minutes before the meeting was scheduled to begin.

"Got any idea what this meeting is all about?" asked Sandberg, desperately trying to suppress the cheerfulness from his voice. He had heard Hofstead make one too many references about Florida not to suspect what was coming. He stretched in front of Swenson and dropped an empty folder at the place immediately to the left of Hofstead's presumed seat, and with measured nonchalance proceeded to the coffee maker.

Swenson blinked at the table for a few seconds and announced, "You know, I think I've already had too much coffee today." He proceeded to slide Sandberg's empty folder down the table, replace it with his own folder, bulging with computer printouts, and sit down with his empty "Hofstead Hail" coffee mug. He continued pleasantly, "I don't expect the meeting to last too long. You see, I've been providing him with material about how we can make our office more efficient and our growth rate stronger through the extensive use of advanced software. I'm sure he just wants to speak to all of us together about these plans."

Returning with his coffee, Sandberg lugubriously eyed the table. He realized he had no choice but to sit down, pretend he didn't notice, and remember the tactic. The next eight and a half minutes were taken up with staid, frosty, and fatuous communications about the weather while Swenson wondered if he dared to get up for that cup of coffee for which he was ready to kill.

Thirty seconds before the meeting was to begin, Mrs. Kvamme came in with a steno pad and several manila folders containing sales and actuarial figures. Both men were delighted to see her as a welcome relief from seeing each other.

"What's this all about, Borghild?" inquired Clarence Sandberg. "The last time we met in here was when John gave us his United Way pep talk. Has he volunteered us to clean up the litter along a mile of highway or something?"

Borghild scowled and replied, "There's nothing I can tell you, I'm afraid. He's been hiding in his office for a long time, making phone calls. When I asked him the purpose of the meeting he just said 'Wait and see!'"

"Maybe it has something to do with the profits from last year," ventured Gary Swenson. "We had a good year. We sold a lot of insurance and mother nature was on our side. I know I sold more insurance than I ever have, and Clarence, you even sold more than usual, didn't you? Maybe he's going to announce a bonus or something. He enjoys pleasant little surprises."

Sandberg was trying to come up with a response to the snide use of the word "even" in Swenson's reference, when he heard Hofstead's door opening. Hofstead glanced in to see that Myron Pekanen was not yet seated and walked over to retrieve the latecomer. It was with a degree of repressed joy that Swenson and Sandberg heard the annoyance in Hofstead's voice as he said, "Come on, Pek. You're late!"

This was followed by a somewhat addled, "Huh? Is it three o'clock already? Yah, I'll get my cup and be right there."

Hofstead preceeded Pekanen into the room and pulled out the chair at the head of the table. "Sit right down here, Pek. I don't intend to keep anyone too long." Sandberg and Swenson tried to avoid looking at each other and failed.

With that, Hofstead sat down on the other side of Borghild, folded his hands in front of him, and, enjoying every minute of the suspense he had created, said, "I suppose you are wondering why I called you all together." To John Hofstead, it was the perfect cliché.

Nobody spoke, and Hofstead continued to beam at them in all his radiant pinkness. After ten seconds of bewildered silence, Myron Pekanen said, "Yeah, so, what's up?"

"Ha!" said Hofstead with undisguised glee, "thought you'd never ask! I'm quitting!"

"Er, ah, quitting what?" asked the deliberate but hopeful Clarence Sandberg.

"Quitting business. Quitting work. Quitting the rat race. Quitting getting up at six thirty every morning. Quitting spending my winters in Minnesota. In short, I quit!"

Four minds immediately turned to their own futures. "But," protested Swenson, "you can't just quit!"

"Why not?" said the grinning pink eminence.

"Well, I mean, ah, well, what's to become of the company?" Swenson inquired cautiously.

"Yes, well, you see, that's where you come in."

A stunned but elated expression spread across Swenson's face. "Me?"

"Yah, you. And Clarence. And Pek. And maybe even Borghild if she would consider it."

"What, er, just what is it you mean?" spluttered Clarence Sandberg.

Hofstead leaned back in his chair and beamed. "You see, I've been running this business a long time, and as I see it, if I'm gonna quit, I got two choices. I can sell the business to whoever wants it at the best price I can get and go away and never think about it again. And maybe that's what I should do. But, you know, when you spend your whole life doing something, it isn't so easy just to walk away from it. So I don't want to do that. Instead, I'm gonna own the company, but I'm just not gonna run the company. I'm still gonna own the company, but instead of being president, I'm going to be your chief executive officer." Hofstead paused and smirked, "Your CEO! And I don't intend to do a lick of work. That's where you come in. I intend to hire one of you to be my president."

Hofstead let those words hang in the air like a bountiful piñata, ready to pour blessings down upon a chosen one. Clarence Sandberg looked at his co-workers, and noted with dread the smug expression on the face of Swenson. Borghild Kvamme also looked at her co-workers, and dreaded the thought that one of them would probably be her future boss. Gary Swenson looked confidently at John Hofstead, attempting to convey a message that said, "I'm ready for this, and you know that I'm your man!" Myron Pekanen looked at the rubber band he had unconsciously wrapped around his little finger to the point where it had cut off all circulation.

"Yes, it will be one of you, all right," the new self-appointed CEO continued, "but I haven't made up my mind which one. I presume you would all like the job. I wouldn't hire you and keep you on all these years if I thought you were the kind of people who would shrink from a challenge or an opportunity. Now, Clarence, you've been with me longer than anyone else. You know the business and would make a good president. Pek? When you joined the company, business just took off and we haven't looked back since. You brought in a lot of policies from territories that we had never even considered. Gary? What can I say? You've been the leading salesman for the last five years. And Borghild? Well, everybody knows who really runs Hofstead Hail, huh?"

Everyone patronizingly chuckled as Borghild smiled in the manner she was expected to and blushed appropriately.

"So. It won't be an easy choice. Since I own the business and I still want to make enough money to pay my Florida greens fees," he paused to grin from one person to the other, "I want to hire the right person. I don't want to go outside the company because I'm sure that I've got the right person right here, right now. You all bring special strengths to the company, and maybe each one of you would make a good president. As owner, I know what each of you can do for the company now. But I don't know what you can do in the future. If the new president is not Sandberg, for instance, I want the new president to make use of Sandberg's talents."

("What talents?" thought one person at the table.)

"If the new president of the company is not Pekanen, I want the new president to realize what an asset Pek is to the company and treat him well."

("Treat him to severance pay," thought two people at the table.)

"If the new president is not Swenson, I would hope that he would have enough sense to do everything he could to retain a terrific insurance man."

("Fat chance!" thought three people at the table.)

"Finally, if the new president is not Mrs. Kvamme," ("How nice of him to be so inclusive, and isn't that just like John," thought everybody at the table) "anyone who would not retain her would have to have rocks in his head.

"I've taken pride in the fact that I put together a darn good insurance team here. In running this outfit, I've seen what each of you can bring to the company and since I still intend to make my living off of the profits of Hofstead Hail. Yes, the name will not change. Whoever I select will have to demonstrate that he—or she, of course—can work with the remaining members."

Four pairs of eyes looked at the speaker and each pair peeked surreptitiously at the other three. Each member of the firm was concerned with one major question.

"Now, you're probably asking yourself, 'How's he going to decide this?' Well, I'll tell you. I don't know. But I'm going to find out. For the last hour I have been making arrangements for all of us to go to the Otter Slide Resort for one of their Winter Wonderland specials. You know the place. It's on Long Lake just outside of Vergas. Your wives are specifically requested to come along, and

Borghild, I want to make sure you get Harry to come along with you. Martha and I will look forward to spending more time with you in a relaxed setting where we can just unwind and have fun. I mean, they've got cross-country skiing, snowmobiling, ice fishing, tobogganing, sleigh rides with real horses if you give 'em enough warning—the whole nine yards. And, just for you, Pek, they've even got a sauna. Now, maybe you're not the active type—well, that's okay, too. Just bring a good book and sit and relax. All meals are included and it's all on me.

"Now, I didn't have a whole lot of choice when it came to dates, so I just picked January twenty-eighth through January thirtieth. I realize that doesn't leave you with much time to plan. But you don't need to plan for anything. Just show up. I expect you to cancel any other plans you may have and be there. I asked them to send us some brochures on the place that will tell you everything you will need to know."

Hofstead stood up and folded his hands at the point where his vest met his trousers, and in the process made his tummy look like a bowling trophy.

"So. That's about it! Meeting adjourned! Gosh, this was fun! I can hardly wait to get home and break the news to Martha."

TWO

"I swear," said Deputy Orly Peterson, ostentatiously crossing his heart. "That's the way it was. I heard it from a Douglas County deputy who was there when they fished him out."

"There wasn't anything about that in the official report, or even in the papers," protested Sheriff Palmer Knutson. "You'd think a story like that would get picked up by the newspapers, at least."

"Yeah, well, if you had chucked your fishing spear into a body you might have been a little reluctant to brag about it, wouldn't you?"

"You mean," the sheriff blinked, "he actually hit him?"

"Yeah, sort of. That's how they kept the body from drifting any further and could keep him until they got the sheriff down there. I guess it didn't really hit the body, but the spear caught in the hood of the parka the guy had on." The deputy smirked. "I can see it now. Somebody asks him, 'Catch anything today?' and he says, 'You bet, I got a hundred-and-seventy-five-pound Norwegian!'"

It was a period of quiet for Fergus Falls and all of Otter Tail County. The Christmas holidays were over and the big Crazy Days sale at the Westridge Mall had come and gone. The Lutheran Brethren School's Annual World Mission Conference was going to be held soon, but the chances of that inaugurating a wave of crime were not high. In fact, nothing was high. The average high temperature for the month of January in Fergus Falls is eight above zero, and this winter seemed to be below average. Burglaries are always down in January because nobody wants to stand outside jimmying a lock when one's hands freeze to the doorknob and every bit of minor villainy can be followed up by tracks in the snow. So it was a time to catch up on old cases and read about crime and crime prevention in other less blessed communities. It was a time to consider, and abandon, plans for redecorating the office. And it was a time to listen to Deputy Orly Peterson.

Knutson blinked through his too-round, horn-rimmed glasses. He had selected the frames all by himself, without the help of his esthetically sensitive wife. He thought the frames had made him look wise, something that was always an asset in an elective office.

Ellie, however, had unkindly remarked, "Wise? Yes, I can see that. What, after all, is the symbol of Athens? The symbol of wisdom itself? An owl. The only thing missing is a mouse in your beak."

The worst thing was, after the seed had been planted in his mind, every time he looked at himself in the mirror he felt like hooting.

Palmer Knutson had long considered himself to be in his middle ages, but had recently accepted that the term "late middle ages" was more appropriate. He preferred a relaxed atmosphere in his office and today he was wearing a heavy woolen, official British Navy-surplus sweater. His daughter, who attended Concordia College, had gone off on a May seminar in London and brought him back this treasured souvenir. It had patches on the shoulders and on the elbows and looked like something James Bond would put on for night duty. The dark blue set off his light blue eyes and his reddish blond hair, blending into gray, and strategically combed to camouflage a receding hair line. Unfortunately, the sweater was rather tight around the middle and tended to accentuate the round bulges hanging over his belt. Palmer lugubriously eyed the stretched fabric at his midsection and regretted the lefse and rommegrot and Christmas cookies that he had so enthusiastically and thoughtlessly consumed.

"You know," he resumed, after allowing Orly his enjoyment of the concept of fishing for Norwegians, "the annual Sertoma Fishing Derby is coming up on Pebble Lake. That sort of thing could happen to us. Are you prepared to go out and handle something like that without making jokes about it?"

Orly Peterson, who at least looked the part of a deputy, resented the implication. Although his status would have allowed him to do at least some work in plain clothes, he seldom appeared in anything but his spotless and carefully pressed tan and brown uniform. And always, even on a cold day in January when he had nowhere to go but the restroom, he wore his nine-millimeter 92F Beretta strapped to his side. He worked out regularly and had, in the sheriff's opinion, a disgustingly small amount of body fat on his six-foot frame. Besides, the uniform was the perfect complement to his closely cut brown hair and his soft brown eyes. Knutson had once teased him that he wore his uniform because he thought it would appeal to women. He could tell by the way his deputy blushed that he had made a direct hit. But Orly was offended by Knutson's newest dig.

"Of course I could handle it! Have I ever given you any reason to think that I couldn't?"

In truth, Knutson was hard-pressed to remember any incident when that was the case and mumbled a vague apology.

"But what happened there, anyway?" asked Peterson, appropriately forgiving the slight by ignoring the issue. "Did they ever find out how come he fell in the lake in the first place?"

"Funny you should ask," replied the sheriff, suppressing a grin. "Just after it happened I got a call from Loyal Rue, the Douglas County sheriff. He thought he had a murder on his hands. It seems that when they fished the corpse out of the hole in the ice they were able to identify who it was. They found the poor sap's fish house only a hundred yards away, and tried to get in, but the door was locked from the inside."

"I thought that was illegal?"

"It is. You're not even supposed to have locks on the inside. But he did, and for reasons best known to himself he had locked the door. Well, anyway, they bring the victim back and the county coroner finds a deep bruise on the side of his head. So Rue decides maybe someone whacked him with a blunt instrument and he thinks he's got himself a locked-room murder. I mean, he even suggested a frog man in a wet suit had popped out of the fishing hole and done him in."

Peterson leaned forward and Knutson could spot the "Oh, I wish we could get a case like that" look in his eyes. He commented before the deputy had a chance to voice his envy. "You know how everybody in Alexandria is sort of jealous of us in everything?" the sheriff continued, revealing a deeply felt and widely held Fergus Falls attitude. "Well, I guess since we had that Gherkin murder last year Rue has always felt that he has to keep up. He said he wanted to consult with me. Well, what was I supposed to tell him? All I could do was assure him that it wasn't the same murderer. Anyway, before that went any further they discovered that their victim had been overcome by carbon monoxide gas. The fool had built a little fire in his stove and had not checked the chimney, which was filled up with snow. He just fell asleep and toppled into the hole, and in the process had bumped his head. Rue called me back later to tell me about it, but I never heard about the spear."

"Yeah, well, that's how they got him out. Can you imagine? You're sitting in a dark fish house with a spear in one hand and a bottle of bourbon in the other. You see something in the hole and you strike! You pull in the line and what do you have? A Norwegian! That reminds me ..."

Knutson winced. It looked like Peterson was about to tell another Norwegian joke. It wasn't that Palmer didn't like Norwegian jokes, but he only liked them when they were told by a fellow Norwegian. Peterson was a Swede, and a supercilious one at that. "Or is it a redundancy to call a Swede supercilious?" Knutson thought as he prepared for the worst.

"So there's this big construction project in Minneapolis, see. And there's a German and an Italian and Ole working up on the forty-ninth floor. And it's lunch break, see, and the German opens his lunch box and cries, '*Ach du Lieber*! Sauerkraut again! If I get sauerkraut in my lunch one more time I'm going to walk off the top of this here building.' And then the Italian opens up his lunch bucket and he yells out 'Mama Mia! It'sa spaghetti again! If I see spaghetti one more time ina my luncha box I'ma gonna jump offa the topa thisa building.' And sure enough, Ole, he opens up his box and says, 'Uffda! Lefse! Lefse again. If I get lefse in my lunch one more time I tink I'm going to yump off dis building.'

"So the next day, of course, the German opens up his lunch box and says '*Ach du Lieber*' when he sees the sauerkraut and walks off the top of the building, and he falls all the way down and he gets killed. And sure enough, the Italian opens his lunch, sees the spaghetti. 'Mama Mia,' he says and off he goes. Then Ole, he opens up his lunch and sure enough, there's the lefse, so he says 'Uffda' and off he goes."

Peterson sat back while Knutson tried but failed to see the point of the story. After an overlong pause, Peterson continued, "Then they had to have a funeral, you know."

"Yah, go on," the sheriff patiently replied.

"Well, everybody was crying and stuff and the German widow was just inconsolable. 'Why didn't he tell me he didn't want sauerkraut?' she asked. 'I thought he loved it. For twenty-three years he loved it!' 'I know just what you mean,' said the Italian woman. 'I gave my husband spaghetti every day for nineteen years because he told everyone what a wonderful wife I was to give him his spaghetti every day.' Well, then, they both looked over at Lena. She looked back at them and said, 'Don't look at me! Ole always packed his own lunch!'"

By the time he finished the punch line, Orly was laughing hard at his own joke. Palmer, however, pushed up his glasses with his knuckle and said, "But if all three of them jumped down and died, how did the widows know the reason for their suicide?"

Orly stared at him for fifteen seconds and finally said, "Apparently there were more men than just those three on the 49th floor. Men who were infinitely satisfied with their noon repast and did not feel the need to commit suicide. More than likely these men, who of course had tried to prevent the suicides to the best of their citizen responsibility but who had failed in this endeavor, and who had shamefacedly admitted their inability to prevent the collective deaths, had reported the circumstances to the local law enforcement agencies who had referred them to individual trauma counselors. Geez!" The deputy shook his head and returned to his own office.

"That's a funny joke," Palmer thought. "I gotta tell that to Ellie when I get home." The sheriff smiled as he anticipated his wife's rich and deep giggle. But over the course of the next minute, the smile faded and a furrow spread across his brow. Did the Douglas County sheriff really envy Knutson for his opportunity to solve a murder? No one, he thought, could ever willingly want to deal with the sadness, suspicion, and horror that murder called forth.

"No," he said to himself, "that was the first murder in Otter Tail County in several decades. We'll probably get through several more before we have another one. By then, who knows? Maybe Orly will be the sheriff."

As Knutson smiled at the thought of Orly as the county "man of the law," passions and circumstances moved inexorably to prove his prediction to be very wrong.

THREE

Iris Pekanen pulled out a long dress from her closet, sniffed the armpit, brushed some lint from the velvet top and asked, "Honey, do you think I should take this along this weekend?"

Myron Pekanen, who had learned never to render a direct judgment on his wife's clothes, demurred, "If you like."

"I mean, do you think there would be an occasion to wear a long dress at the resort? We will be dining together, won't we?" Her tinny voice rose with each interrogative, as it did at the end of every sentence, for that matter.

"I don't know, I suppose so. 'Pinky' didn't say. In fact, all I know about the weekend is that we are supposed to be there tonight and, according to him, 'be prepared to enjoy ourselves.'" Pek held up a 1.75 liter bottle of Black Velvet Canadian, lovingly admired the label, and with an affection born of long years of intimacy, tenderly placed it into the suitcase. "I think I can handle that."

"But what's the restaurant like? Will the other wives wear long dresses? I mean, it's a swanky place, after all."

"I don't know," Pek grunted. "Maybe they will. But you know, even though it's sort of expensive, it's still a resort. I've never been in a resort restaurant yet where people get real dressed up."

"Since your experience with resort restaurants only runs to 'Shorty's Muskie Heaven' on Lake Winnibigoshish, I don't find that too comforting. This is a 'retreat center.' All the big executives from Northwest Airlines and 3M come up for conferences. I don't want to ruin your chances of being president of Hofstead Hail by showing up in something dowdy."

In a brief spasm of mental ambition, Pek tried to think of anything his wife had that wasn't dowdy. Giving it up, he wheezed a patient sigh, "Well, take it along, then."

"But if I take that along, then I'll have to take along other shoes and another bag."

Without protest or a hint of recrimination, Pek said, "I'll go down and get the big suitcase."

An objective but unkind person may have wondered if thoughtful preparations would really make a difference for Iris Pekanen. She was a short and dumpy woman who had "let herself go" after the birth of her third child. A skilled glamour photographer might have been able to do something with her short, straight, mousy brown hair, but it would have strained his creativity. She used to wear contact lenses and used eye makeup to call attention to her bright, if tiny, blue eyes, but all of that just gradually became too much trouble. As an insurance salesman, her husband had to do his share of traveling, and, befitting his stature as the subject of many a dirty joke, he had never been faithful to her for very long. Of course, she didn't know this, and the trusting soul was content with life. As she sucked in her breath and straightened her posture in front of the mirror, however, she decided that if she were going to be the wife of an executive, she really should look the part. Aloud, she declared to herself, "The diet begins on Monday!"

Pek, who returned with a huge piece of ancient Samsonite just in time to hear this proclamation, did not let it pass. Without cruel intent, but with no sensitivity whatsoever, he observed, "I've heard that before. It's never worked before and I doubt if it will work now. You are what you are."

In this case, the philosophy defined the man. Myron Pekanen clung tightly to the Greek dictum of "know thyself" and was never dissatisfied with the man he knew. He was of pure Finnish stock, the product of immigrants who had made the passage from Finland to Michigan's Upper Peninsula to the farming areas of New York Mills, Minnesota. He was not tall, but was powerfully built and had a swarthy complexion that set him apart from the "Swede-Finns." His dark eyebrows grew out of a forehead that seemed to have a perpetual swelling and made his dark eyes appear romantic, sensual, and, totally at variance with the facts, intellectually alive. It was an interesting face, but the wide, flat nose unconditionally disqualified him from ever being called handsome. He accepted this, just as he accepted his wife's appearance. He knew she was dumpy, and merely assumed that she knew it too. If he could accept it, he figured she should also.

"No, really, Pek. I mean it. I want you to be proud of me." Before her husband could respond with yet another insensitive remark, she continued, "I've always thought that Mrs. Hofstead carries herself with such poise and style. I want to be just like her when you are president of the firm. And I'm going to start being like that from now on, because you, dear, are going to be the one. I just know it."

Her husband was studying which two pairs of identical brown socks he should toss in the suitcase. "Well, I suppose Hofstead could pick me to run the company. I could do it, you know."

"Of course you could, dear."

"I mean it," Pek added as he folded up a pair of brown slacks identical to the pair he had on and selected two blue button-down shirts to put into the suitcase. "I've doubled the number of policies sold in this five-county area. I went out and sold hail insurance where they had never even bothered to go before. I've made a lot of money for the company, and Hofstead knows it. He said he was still interested in making money, and I think I'm the one to do it."

Iris, selecting a month's supply of costume jewelry to put into a velvet-covered box, asked, "Of all the others he said he would consider, who, other than yourself, of course, do you think has the best chance?"

Pek sat down on the bed and absentmindedly began to play with the nap of the velvet bedspread. "Clarence, for sure. It's gonna be Clarence. I can make Hofstead more money, but you know him. He has these 'other considerations' that he keeps talking about. I point out how we could increase our sales by just cranking up the pressure on some of these farmers who are underinsured and he just says there are 'other considerations.' Clarence is dull and just a little lazy, but he has been with Hofstead for over thirty years. He can be sure that Clarence will never have an original idea and therefore he can run the company from Florida by making one telephone call a month. That's what he really wants anyhow."

"Oh dear, that means that I'll probably have to spend more time with that tedious Joey Sandberg. What a dumb name for a sixty-year-old woman! Is it short for Josephine or something?"

"Actually, I think it's short for Joanne, which any woman should certainly prefer. But I can't see where you'd have to cozy up to her. Would you prefer it if Borghild were made president? Then you could get together with the number one company spouse and compare recipes with Harry Kvamme."

This rare display of wit made Iris smile as she asked, "Do you think there's any chance of that?"

"Nah," Pek snorted, "Hofstead's too smart for that. He knows how valuable she is. If me or Clarence or even Gary were made president, she would still be there to keep the company going, no matter what. That's what I would do. She's already almost a co-president who works for peanuts. I'd keep it that way."

"But what about Gary Swenson?" Iris tentatively asked.

"Gary Swenson, Young Gary," Pek repeated, the sarcasm heavy in his voice. "I don't know. He's young. He is always doing something with that damn computer of his. I swear, I think he takes that Powerbook with him even when he goes to the john. And you can just tell that Hofstead finds that impressive. I've gotta admit that he has put up some good numbers since he joined the company, but I sometimes wonder if he just uses that computer to make the numbers say anything he wants them to. But I can't see Hofstead picking him ahead of Clarence."

"Can you see him picking him ahead of you?"

"I don't know, but I'm sure of one thing. Gary can see himself being picked ahead of both of us. And Borghild? Well, if Young

Gary gets picked as president, she better learn how to run computers better or he'll get rid of her."

Iris sat down next to her husband and put her arm around his neck in a clumsy attempt at intimacy. "Honey, do you think there is anything that we can do to influence this decision?"

"Nah," Pek replied, disentangling himself with a minimum of grace. "I'm not sure I even want the job. But maybe I should, if only for self-preservation. I could run it better than any of them, I think, but I'm not sure I could work under somebody like Young Gary. I think I'll see if I can get a private word with Hofstead sometime this weekend. He likes to snowmobile and that's provided as part of the 'Winter Wonderland Weekend.' I know the territory around Vergas. Maybe I can get him alone and make my pitch."

"Well, I've always thought that Martha has rather liked me," Iris optimistically proclaimed as she closed her suitcase. "I'll have to drop a few hints to her about how the insurance company would be in good hands with you."

"All right, but don't use that expression."

"What?"

"The 'good hands,' you know, for insurance."

"Why not?"

"Never mind," Pek sighed. "Are you packed and ready to go?"

"All ready. Do I look presentable?"

"About as presentable as you'll get, I suppose. I'll put the big suitcase in the car so we can leave as soon as your mother gets here."

"Wasn't it sweet of her to agree to come and spend the weekend with the kids? We really ought to spend more time with her."

"One of us should, anyway," Pek mumbled.

"What did you say, Pek?"

"I just said, 'Yeah, we should.'"

FOUR

THE SUN WAS LOW on the snowy horizon to the left of Clarence Sandberg's beige Oldsmobile as he drove north on Highway 59. It was one of those lifeless afternoons in Minnesota, when the sundogs guard the flanks of a sun without warmth. As he passed through Erhard, he fine-tuned his radio to "The Mighty 790" KFGO radio from Fargo, North Dakota. A Garth Brooks tune was just beginning, but as he opened his mouth to provide the country singer with a monotone duet, his wife of twenty-nine years, Joey, chose that moment to say, "Do you think John will make us go snowmobiling?"

It was a question that deserved an answer, and Clarence reluctantly turned down the volume and said, "Well, I'm sure that he won't make you do anything you don't want to do. He just wants us to have a good time. It might be fun."

"Fun? To sit on a machine that makes as much noise as those stupid Shriners motorcycles do at the parades? I hate those things. And I can just picture a bunch of Shriners doing figure eights on snowmobiles if they ever held a winter parade. So we should run around like a bunch of Shriners in the woods scaring the living daylights out of the squirrels while we freeze our fannies? If that's what it takes for you to become president of the company I suppose I can do it for a while, but don't expect me to call it fun. And I suppose I have to sit there in my good coat and get it torn up by the machinery."

"No, no. No chance of that. The Otter Slide Resort supplies the whole outfit—snowmobile suits, helmets, boots, and even mittens. Besides, nobody's going to make you go. You can sit around and read a book if you want to."

"Sure, and have John think, 'Clarence is a good man, but his wife is sure a stick in the mud. She wouldn't help him sell insurance if she couldn't get out and enjoy a Minnesota winter.' I've spent fifty-nine winters in Minnesota and I've never enjoyed a one of them, but that doesn't mean I complain about them."

"No, not much it doesn't," thought Clarence, but aloud he said, "Well, I say, don't knock it if you haven't tried it. I've never been on a snowmobile either, but I'm kind of looking forward to it. Would you rather try cross-country skiing?"

"At my age? Don't be absurd!"

"What do you mean, at your age? You're not so old. The Otter Slide provides everything you need. It's supposed to be much easier than downhill skiing and a lot safer. Or, hey! I know! How about coming ice fishing with me?"

Joey's voice was colder than a well-digger's heel as she said, "There is only one thing more stupid than sitting out in a boat catching fish that nobody ever eats. And that is sitting in a dark fish house on a frozen lake trying to catch fish that nobody ever eats. No thank you!"

"Yah, maybe," Clarence tentatively agreed, "but that's not the point. In any event, it's still a nice gesture, you know. It's just a real pleasant way for John to get us all together and make us all comfortable with each other when he goes and I'm the new president."

He let his mind wander to the future. He was a contented man who was essentially satisfied with life. Hofstead Hail had been good to him. He had sent one daughter to Concordia College and the other daughter was a senior at Gustavus Adolphus College. His two hundred and fifty pounds were spread inelegantly on his six-foot-two frame and his massive, bespectacled, and clean-shaven face hid not a trace of guile. His protruding ears held up a fur hat covering a scalp the adornment of which was summed up in his favorite bumper sticker, "Don't say bald, say 'combing impaired!'" He lived the life of an isolated Swede in a sea of Norwegians—he got along, he went along, and he didn't make waves.

Joey was, in many ways, the perfect complement to Clarence. She, too, was large, and in no way physically attractive. Her idea of glamour, and a not altogether mistaken one in her case, was to appear sensibly dressed and clean at all times. She could never understand the attraction of shopping at Nordstrom's when there was a perfectly acceptable ensemble to be had at Penney's. Her brown hair was styled in a short permanent wave and hadn't changed since the day they married. Her blue eyes, somewhat magnified behind large eyeglasses in a frame dating to the Carter administration, were warm and surrounded by the pleasant wrinkles often referred to as "laugh lines." They had always been a very respectable couple. After five minutes of pleasant silence, she said, "So you think you will be, then?"

"Will be what, Joey?"

"The new president. That's what this is all about, isn't it? I'd hate to think I am subjecting myself to a full weekend with that dreadful Iris Pekanen for nothing. It sounds like a beauty contest with you and Pek and Gary waltzing down the runway while some washed-up celebrity judges appreciate your loveliness."

Clarence did not allow his mind to dwell on that image. "Now, Joey. You know it won't be anything like that. John just wants us to build togetherness so that the business can function without him. I think it will be a good thing and valuable when I'm president."

"So you have no doubts about that, huh? What about Borghild? She knows as much about the company as you do and has been with him longer."

"Well, you know, me and John are the same age almost. We grew up in a different era. We're used to having a woman as our secretary, not as our boss. I think many of our policy holders would probably feel the same way. Now you know me, I'm all for women's rights and everything, but in this business you can't afford to be a leader in anything."

Joey nodded ruefully and thought, "If that's the case, you are certainly qualified for the job." Aloud she said, "What about Pek?"

"No, no, no. Certainly not. I mean, Pek's all right. He brings in a lot of business. But he's kind of a sneaky type, if you know what I mean. None of the Norwegians or Swedes would ever trust a Finn. And he does like his booze. People claim he never sells a policy without capping it off with a snort. No, I think John likes him just where he is."

"And Young Gary?"

"To tell you the truth," Clarence said, his face perceptibly darkening, "I'm a little afraid of Gary. I think John is, too. Anytime anybody brings anything up, Gary whizzes into his office and pretty soon you hear that 'ticky-ticky-ticky' from his computer and the next thing you know he's shoving a spreadsheet under your nose and saying 'See, I told you I was right.' Now, I don't know if he is right or not, because that stuff is all a mystery to me, but I also know it is a mystery to John. I see his eyes glaze over the same way mine do and he cuts him off with an enthusiastic 'nice work, Gary' and quickly says, 'How about those Vikings?'"

Clarence adjusted his safety belt from one roll of fat to another and continued, "Still, John knows how to read the bottom line, and the agency has really done well since Gary joined. The way I see it, John will see me as president until I decide to retire, oh happy day, and then Gary can take over for me. I figure, what the heck, I could easily tolerate Gary working for me, but John's gotta know I couldn't work for Gary."

"I'm sure you're right, Clarence, but I'll just try to get Martha aside for a while this weekend and see if she knows which way the wind is blowing. We've always had a nice relationship and she always tells me anything she knows."

"And I'm going to have a little heart-to-heart with John. I won't ask him for anything, I don't think that would be proper. But I would like to reminisce about the last twenty-five years and share with him the way I see Hofstead Hail shaping up over the next twenty-five. Continuity is a good thing, you know. Maybe we'll just go off on our snowmobiles and talk the whole thing over like we used to do."

This was already more conversation than Clarence was used to, and he leaned forward to turn up the volume on the radio, thus signaling to Joey that the topic had been exhausted. An overly familiar song by Billy Ray Cyrus provided diversion for the last mile of the trip.

FIVE

With a master touch gained from hours spent working on his computer keyboard, Gary Swenson punched out his home number on his desk telephone, a device cleverly shaped to resemble a Porsche Targa. With the windshield to his ear and the sloping trunk in front of his mouth, the effect would have been worth at least one major conference paper for a Freudian psychologist. As he pictured his wife's camera cell phone ringing at home, he impatiently wondered why Faye Janice was taking so long to answer. At last he heard a breathless, "The Swenson-Nelson residence."

"Faye Janice? It's me. Are you ready? What were you doing?"

"I was in the bathroom, if you must know, and yes, I've been ready for some time. You said you wanted to leave at four o'clock and it is now a quarter to five. Are we still planning to go?"

"Of course. I was just running off a little data on how we can improve efficiency by paying off on all claims on two set days of the month instead of the piecemeal way we've always done it. I wanted to bring these figures along this weekend and show them to Hofstead. What I was calling about was that I wanted to make sure you packed our ski gear."

"Our ski gear? You want I should put the skis in the rack?"

"No, no," Swenson replied, his condescension all too apparent, "we aren't going downhill skiing. That's too violent for this crowd. But there is some talk about cross-country skiing and it appears that everyone is going snowmobiling. I just thought that we should have our thermal long-johns and socks packed, and that perhaps a set of aprés-ski wear would be nice if we have any social time in the lounge. What do you think?"

"I've already packed our Norwegian sweaters; I thought that would please Hofstead. But I was going to ask if you thought we should take our bathing suits. They do have a pool at that resort, don't they?"

"To tell you the truth, I doubt it. Swimming is a big thing in the summer, of course, but that is what the lake is for. But I do remember that they mentioned a sauna. When's the last time we took a sauna together?"

"Not long ago enough. I can never see the charm of sitting there sweating like a butcher and having my makeup run and have all the curl wilt out of my hair."

"Yah, but look at the bright side. We could get to keep Pek and Iris company, har-har. You can bet he'll be there. That's the sort of thing that makes his little Finnish heart go 'thumpity-thump.' I wonder if he'd rather sit next to you in your swimsuit than Iris in hers. That thought boggles the mind."

"It boggles my mind that I would welcome a chance to sit and sweat next to Pek. But anyway, I thought they didn't wear swim suits in their saunas."

"Hey, that's right. Oh boy, a chance to see Iris, that shapeless mound of cellulite, in the altogether. Uffda." Gary Swenson and Faye Janice Nelson always enjoyed their mutual and shared smugness. They were in their early thirties with no children and were the type of people who had done very nicely from carefully selected tech stocks. They prided themselves on their posture, workout habits, and healthy eating. They had once been introduced to social responsibility in college, and discovered that they just didn't care for it.

Gary believed that the clothes make the man. It is always easy for nice clothes to look elegant on a mannequin, and Gary was able to adopt the mannequin's mien as well as its soul. He had pleasant blue eyes that always seemed to shine more than was physically normal. His teeth seemed unnaturally white, his nose unnaturally straight, his blond hair unnaturally coiffed. He wore a tan cashmere topcoat to work, but for his Winter Wonderland Weekend he was planning to change to his informal Eddie Bauer down parka.

Professionally he had done well at Hofstead Hail. It wasn't that he had a salesman's personality—many of his policy holders, in fact, rather distrusted his outward perfection—but he did have a cunning sense of when to sell. He studied weather patterns of previous years and previous days and often showed up just after a small hailstorm had frightened the uninsured farmer. Armed with the latest long-range forecasts, he often made a sale where even John Hofstead had failed. And he owed it all to his computer.

Nobody doubted his wizardry at his iMac, and Swenson would make no decision without consulting it. An end-product of his trust in computers was his Saab 9-3. He fed all the information about cars he could find into his computer and it proved to his entire satisfaction that it was the smartest car to buy in terms of value, safety, performance, and versatility. Of course, one might note that he had always wanted a Saab in the first place, so that the type of data he put into the computer may have had something to do with the final results. In fact, one could probably say that about most of the things for which Gary used his computer. But no one said so out loud, at least not around Hofstead Hail, where Gary and his technically advanced super sales kept John in awe and the rest in envy.

Faye Janice was in many ways the female version of Gary. Her collection of exercise videos was the most complete to be found in Minnesota, and they were treated with such reverence that if they had been books, they would have been signed first editions. She did, in fact, have a signed letter from Jane Fonda, which was treasured as though it were an original of *Magna Carta.*

Ever since her parents had contrived the name it was always "Faye Janice," with the first name never being used alone. Even in their most intimate moments Gary whispered the entire name. A stranger might wonder why this was so, but once acquaintance was made it became apparent that no other appellation was sufficient. She was obsessed with the subject of body fat, and one would have been hard pressed to find any on her supple, lithe, and athletic body. Her light brown hair, highlighted with a little artificial auburn, was cut so as not to interfere with her workouts and did not really require the ubiquitous headband that always seemed to match her sweat suit. Her facial features were attractive mostly because she knew how to use makeup. In fact, her brown eyes were ordinarily rather dull, so that it was somewhat disconcerting to notice that while her body danced, her eyes didn't.

She had a part-time job teaching women's physical education at Fergus Falls State University, a not altogether demanding position that allowed her to keep her home up to the standards that would reflect well on her husband's climb up the ladder of success in "the insurance industry." Even now, as she talked to him on the telephone, she was thinking that when Gary became president of Hofstead Hail she would have to redo the living room to make it more presentable to important clients. After all, with Gary's direction, the number of "insurance products" offered to "customers" was projected to increase significantly.

As she wandered around the house with her telephone, Faye Janice asked, "You don't think Hofstead was serious when he indicated that all four of you were under real consideration for the presidency of the company, do you?"

Gary flicked a speck of earwax from the windshield of the little Porsche and chuckled, "No, of course not. Can you picture a letterhead proclaiming 'Myron Pekanen: President'? No way. And I'm sure he was just being nice to Borghild. She's hardly executive material, and she's barely mastered the word processor. I figure he might play it safe and pick Clarence for old time's sake. I think he has a hang-up about young people, and I think he equates us with those tiresome people of the sixties. I mean, Pek is not far removed from that generation, but he doesn't seem to feel threatened by him. Nevertheless, if he is serious about making money and running the business as it should be run in the twenty-first century, well, I've just got a feeling that you'll be going to bed every night with the president of Hofstead Hail."

"What if it's Clarence?"

"In that case, I hope you prefer someone other than the president of Hofstead Hail. Look, I'll just gather my papers together and I'll be home in fifteen minutes. We'll get to the Otter Slide just in time to freshen up for dinner. Ta-ta, love."

"Ta-ta, love," Faye Janice echoed.

SIX

Harry Kvamme stamped the snow off his shoes in the entry of his aging home and carefully hung up his parka. He proceeded into the kitchen, wheezed as he sat down, and stared at his feet. After a solemn moment, he slowly began unlacing his heavy work boots. Quite unnecessarily, he announced in his lilting Norwegian brogue, "Borghild, I'm home."

Harry had left work early that day, a respite that made him appreciate all the more the fact that he was ever closer to retirement from the Fergus Falls Building Center. He had worked there for almost forty years, back in the days when it had simply been called "Wahl's Lumber Yard." He had never gotten used to the change, and distrusted the new easy-to-use products that were the glory of the do-it-yourselfers. He still loved the smell of freshly sawed pine, and hated the odor of plastic. The thought of taking off his comfortable coveralls and flannel shirt and putting on his "dress pants and oxford shoes" depressed him, but he had agreed to accompany Borghild on the Winter Wonderland Weekend, and since Hofstead

Hail was footing the bill, he figured he could put up with white-collar workers for a couple of days if it meant free food. Harry was sixty-two, but his unruly white hair and red nose made him look seventy-two, and sometimes at the end of the day he felt like he was eighty-two. Yet, there was a consistency to be found in the kindness in his light blue eyes and the gentleness in his calloused hands. He loved his wife, and if this was going to be important to Borghild, then by golly it was going to be important to him. He figured he could take anything as long as they didn't try to get him to go out cross-country skiing or snowmobiling or something like that. He had already packed his ice fishing gear in the car and if worse came to worse, he could always retreat to an ice fishing house.

As he contemplated his toes, comfortably nestled in his thick woolen socks, Borghild came into the kitchen and said, "I've already packed your things. I figured you might like to sneak out for some fishing, so I got you some warm things. I don't think it will be a very formal occasion, except maybe for the meals, but I put in a couple of ties just in case. How soon can you be ready? As you can see, I am all set to go."

Harry looked up and admired his wife. She had been a stunningly beautiful girl when he first met her, with long blond hair and blue eyes, and looking as though she had just come from a Norwegian fjord. She had aged well, he thought, although his love for her made him a rather biased judge. Still, she only needed glasses for work around the office, and although she had "thickened in the middle a little bit," she was still an attractive woman. He smiled and said, "Oh, I s'pose I could be ready in ten minutes, but is dere any coffee left? I need yust a little varm up." The thought of getting it himself never occurred to him, nor, for that matter, to Borghild.

"Yah, there's a little bit in the pot. I'll heat it up in the microwave."

They both watched in silence as the "All Fishermen are Liars" mug rotated in the microwave. As she handed him his coffee, Borghild asked the question she had asked for ten thousand evenings, "Tough day at work?" And Harry answered as he had ten thousand times before, "Nei, it vasn't tew bad." But this time he added, "So Yohn, he's retiring, tew, is he? I sometimes tink dat's a pretty good idea."

Borghild nodded and said, "Sometimes I think maybe I should quit when he does. But I know he wants me to stay on at least for a while. I don't think he really trusts any of those guys to carry on in his place. He told me, he says, 'Borghild, just because Martha and I are going to take it easy, I hope you don't think I'm going to let you quit.' So maybe I'll stay for a couple more years until the new president gets settled."

"Vell, I know one ting, dat place could never get along witout yew. He ought to make yew boss of da whole outfit since yew already run da place."

"Oh now Harry, you know he would never pick his secretary to be president of the company. There are some younger women who do that kind of thing, but I think I'll leave that executive stuff to those liberated gals. I could do it, though, you know. In fact, I think I could do it better than any of those three guys."

Harry noisily slurped his coffee. "So who's he going to pick, den, Clarence Sandberg?"

"Yah, I s'pose it will be Clarence. Those guys go back a long time. But Clarence has always depended on John to tell him what to do. I don't know how he will do as a president."

"Vhat about dat Finn?"

"Pek? Well, he is a good salesman. He knows the business, I'll give him that. I just wonder how he would do left on his own. He likes to have a snort or two at noon the way it is. I just wonder how he would do if he didn't have to worry about John smelling his breath."

Harry took a long drink of coffee, ran it through his widely spaced teeth a couple of times, smacked his lips and asked, "Vhat about Young Gary?"

"Uffda! If John picks him I'm going to have to learn to run that computer a whole lot better, that's for sure. But you know, I don't think John relishes the idea of turning over the company to somebody who is so much younger than he is. He still talks about his one bad experience with radical youth, you know, and I just don't think he trusts anyone under forty."

"Vhat vas all dat stuff all about, den?"

"I'm sure I told you. John talks about it all the time. He was visiting at the University of Iowa and he came face to face with a murderer. He'll never get over that."

"Yah, I s'pose dat vould do it all right." After a pause to appreciate the profundity of his words, Harry sighed and said, "No, I guess I'd better get ready to go den. Da Otter Slide! Vhat a dumb name for a motel!"

SEVEN

JOHN HOFSTEAD WAS ALL ready to go. He had packed his suitcase before he had gone into the office and had given his Cadillac a full tank of gas on the way home. He now sat in the blue plush chair next to the entry, wearing his snowmobile suit over his best charcoal gray business suit. As he listened to Martha's final preparations, with drawers closing and closet doors slamming, he contemplated the weekend to come.

He had designed this weekend to objectively rate the candidates for the presidency, but earlier in the week, as he considered the best way to proceed, he had come to a definite conclusion. He knew who his president would be. All evidence pointed clearly to the best candidate. At first, he considered that, instead of screening his employees, he would use the time to get them used to their new boss. But the more he thought about it, the more he began to consider that announcing his decision would only disappoint the members of the company not selected, and why not get everybody to enjoy themselves on their corporate retreat? Besides, he might change his mind, and, in any event, it just might be enjoyable to see to what lengths they would go to suck up to him. No doubt about it! This had the makings of a great weekend!

"A year from now," he mused, "I'll be playing golf in Fort Meyers. Maybe I should even try scuba diving. Heck, I'm not too old to try something new. If that old Jacques Cousteau fellow could do it, I should be able to do it, too. I suppose I'll miss my snowmobiles, though. Maybe I should have taken my own sled along to the Otter Slide Resort. Nah, as long as they've got some for the guests, I might as well try a different sled. I don't want to go through the trouble of hooking up that trailer anyway. Oh, what is taking that woman so long?"

He called up the stairs: "Marthaaaa. You ready pretty soon?"

Martha, who was having trouble with her hair, yelled down, "Just give me a couple more minutes, John," and gave the left side of her head a cloud of hair spray. Martha was a beautiful woman. She was sixty-five years old and therefore her beauty was of a different sort than that of the Fergus Falls Flying Falcons homecoming queen. Her hair, once honey blond, had acquired just the right shade of "elderly but respectable" tint that her hairdresser provided. Her complexion, always wonderful as provided by nature, was augmented by the craft of Mary Kay. Her blue eyes were highlighted in such a manner as to bring out not only their beauty but their owner's personality. She looked good because she took the trouble to do so, and because, in the absence of children, she had always had plenty of time to practice. It was a tradeoff that she would not have willingly made, but she accepted what God had given her. And that, she decided one day while daydreaming during the sermon at the First Norwegian Lutheran Church, was quite a bit.

She was looking forward to this weekend with the same anticipation that a fourteen-year-old has for her last trip to the dentist to have her braces taken off. She seemed to enjoy the company of all of the wives of John's employees. The key word here was, unfortunately, "seemed." Martha was such a charming, genuine person that none of them could tell that it was always a chore for her to be gracious to each of them. The maintained perkiness of Faye Janice made her tired. The whining earnestness of Iris nauseated her. She had tolerated Joey Sandberg's tiresome platitudes for a quarter of a century, and if she heard another word about her semi-lovely daughters again she would scream! An employer can choose his employees, but an employer's wife had to take what comes with them. She had performed the role of the gracious president's wife so long and so well that she felt she had earned the right to quit along with the president. She held an imaginary glass of champagne to the mirror and toasted herself with "Here's to new friends in Florida!"

She couldn't help but wonder who John had in mind for the new president. It was unusual for him to be so close-mouthed about such matters. Usually he talked over all major decisions with her. This time he had simply announced he was turning over the business to someone else and asked her who she thought it should be. Without a pause Martha had said, "Borghild, of course," but she didn't really think John would accept that. Instead of arguing with her, however, he had merely nodded and said, "hmmmmm."

Downstairs, John was getting warm and was entertaining the idea of taking off his snowmobile suit. Instead, he forgot his discomfort and went on planning for the weekend. "I'm going to act as if they all have a chance. Then, when they have all given me their best pitch, I'll just bring up my choice in an off-handed manner and see how they react. That'll tell me a lot right there. I don't know how Clarence will react if I don't pick him. I suppose he will be hurt. But he'll stay with the company. He doesn't have anywhere else to go. And doggone it, I got to do what's best for the whole company. And then there's Pek. Well, I don't think he really expects to be chosen, but I bet that he thinks he deserves it. And maybe he does. But would I be taking a chance trusting my business to a Finn? The first thing you know he'd get drunk and get in a knife fight. And then where would the business be?

"I suppose the big thing will be how to break the news. I can just see Gary jumping up and down inside his pants. No doubt about it. His innovation in computerizing the business has made a world of difference and he deserves to be rewarded. But, goldarnit, when the other guys joined the company they all added things, too. And would Young Gary provide the harmony that has always been a part of Hofstead Hail? On the other hand, I suppose I will lose him if I don't pick him as president. I'm not sure I can afford that.

"And then there's Borghild. Martha sure thinks she could do the job. And Martha is right, as usual. Borghild knows the score and knows how to work with all three of those guys. I wonder if she would even take the job."

Hofstead reached inside his snowmobile suit and scratched his belly. "So, how do I handle this? Should I get them all together and make a big announcement or should I meet with everybody personally first? I rather like the surprise element, I guess, but in any event, I'm going to keep that to myself and not tell anyone, including Martha.

"Uffda, it's getting warm in here. Well, if I'm going to be in Florida, I might as well get used to it. Let's see, when's the last time I spent more than a week away from Minnesota? My gosh, it was that summer I went to that eight-week actuarial seminar at the University of Iowa. Boy, that was sure some experience!"

And John Hofstead let his mind wander back to the summer of 1971. He and Martha had taken over an apartment on Dubuque Street in Iowa City from a graduate student who was doing research in South America. They had been amazed and amused at the changes that had come over college life since their days at Concordia College. John had graduated in the Class of 1956. He had been just a little ashamed of the fact that he had not been in the service to help the boys in Korea. But in Iowa City he found people plotting how to get out of the draft. He had been genuinely alarmed at what he heard about people doctoring up their urine samples or chopping off a toe, lying on their eye charts and faking deafness. He was disgusted to see atheists trying to get into the seminary just to avoid the draft. Still, he had to admit it was an interesting summer. At noon he'd even gone into the Airliner Bar and maybe even into Joe's, with its beery smell and the juke box loudly playing Ike and Tina Turner. He never felt at home in a place like that, but it sure fascinated him.

But as he thought about it, a chill permeated his snowmobile suit. He had seen a murderer. He was on his way to the library one night when a side door opened and a man came running out with such blind fury that he had careened right into him. They both fell to the sidewalk and while they were lying in a heap, the ground shook with an explosion the likes of which he had never heard before or since. The man who ran into him frantically tried to get to his feet and they both stumbled again. This time it seemed he looked deeply into John's face. He had a full beard and hair down to his waist. "A crazy hippy," John had thought at the time.

After the man had gone, John had picked himself up and watched with growing excitement as the police cars, fire trucks, and ambulances came. It was only the next day, as he read an account of the explosion in the *Daily Iowan*, that the full significance of what he had seen became apparent. A librarian had been killed in the explosion, and it was presumed to have been a bomb planted by a radical political group. Indeed, a person with long hair and a beard was seen running from the library just before the bomb went off. My God! He had seen a murderer!

Of course, he had reported everything to the local sheriff's office. "The Johnson County, Iowa, sheriff could sure take a few lessons in manners from Palmer Knutson," he thought in retrospect. But at the time, what could he really say about the suspect other than that he needed a shave and a haircut, and that described just about everybody in Iowa City in those days. Anyway, they finally figured out who he was even though they never caught the guy. Ever since then, John had told the story that there was a murderer out there who knew that John Hofstead was the one man who could place him at the scene of the crime. Things like that never happened at good old Fergus Falls State University, and they'd never happen in a town where Palmer Knutson was sheriff.

At last Martha was ready, and John helped her into her coat. He just couldn't help asking, "So, do you think you can get by with this coat for another couple of months and never buy a winter coat again?"

Martha smiled and zipped up John's snowmobile suit to his chin. "Yes, John," she smiled. "Come Easter time, this coat is going right to the Goodwill store."

EIGHT

"Did you finish checking out the snowmobiles?" asked Sharon Hoffman, as her husband peeled off his parka.

"Yeah, they're all set to go," replied David Hoffman. "That old Polaris runs a little rough, but it will work if we need it. What's the latest count for this weekend?"

"Reservations for five rooms, ten people, same as it was last week at this time. That will at least pay the heating bill for this week, and you know, that's ten more people than we had last year at this time. Nobody ever said this would be an overnight success. And if we can make it through this winter, next winter we will have twice as many."

Sharon and David Hoffman had run the Otter Slide Resort for the last ten years. In that time they had renovated and modernized an old Lutheran Bible camp into a year-round vacation center. It had not been easy. The lakeshore real estate had been their only worthwhile asset, and over the years the rustic cabins had gradually given way to a modern twenty-four-unit motel and restaurant complex. The Hoffman's living quarters occupied part of the west wing of the motel; indeed, the front door to their apartment was accessible through the motel reception area.

Last year, the Otter Slide Restaurant had opened in May to such a resounding success that it became obvious that it could provide a year-round source of revenue. If the restaurant could attract enough customers to stay open, the Hoffmans realized, they could continue to run the motel at little additional expense. No longer would the resort have to depend on the vagaries of Minnesota weather during the three-month period from Memorial Day to Labor Day. During the other nine months, if business was slow, half of the units could be closed. But the new restaurant would stay open and, equipped with an expensive set of room dividers, could provide for the growing demand for conference space.

This had all been Sharon's idea, and with her typical flair and ambition she had already convinced several of Minnesota's leading corporations to hold small group retreats. One such group, from Minnesota Mining and Manufacturing, had spent an entire week at the Otter Slide in late November, and on the basis of 3M's tacit endorsement she had lured other urban corporations as well. In truth, it was an ideal setting for a corporate retreat, with little but snow, wildlife, and a sauna to distract the guests. Shortly before 3M had arrived, Sharon had insisted, over David's reluctance, on the purchase of a fax machine. The company was pleased with the facilities and hinted that next year's retreat might force the Hoffmans to open up the other wing of the motel.

Meanwhile, the Otter Slide Restaurant, which was open only on weekends from January to March unless a conference was being held, was paying the mortgage and the taxes. The menu featured a predictable selection of steaks and chops, but there were speciality items like filet of Minnesota walleye, prairie-fed bison, Minnesota venison, and wild pheasant. But all meals featured a Minnesota speciality. It was not just "a baked potato," for instance, but a "Minnesota Red River Valley Potato." More often than not, however, the diners preferred "genuine Minnesota wild rice, hand-picked by members of the Ojibwe Nation." The fact that much of the wild rice was machine-harvested from non-reservation farms bothered David, but Sharon insisted it was simply a matter of business.

David Hoffman was a chubby-faced, smooth-shaven, elfin sort of a man with a receding chin. His scarce hair was brushed straight back in a futile attempt to hide his baldness, and this pathetic gesture only seemed to make him appear older than his fifty-six years. His serene hazel eyes, magnified by bifocals in black, horn-rimmed glasses, indicated a naiveté that one does not find in successful businessmen. Such an impression was, perhaps, an accurate one, for Hoffman would have created a financial disaster had he been allowed to run the business.

Fortunately, the Otter Slide was not dependent on David Hoffman's business acumen. Sharon Hoffman had the drive, ambition, and imagination to take a disused Bible camp and turn it into a promising enterprise. One had only to watch the couple receive their first paying customer to see where the authority and prospects for success were to be found. Sharon was a take-charge person with a commanding, somewhat unfeminine voice that could welcome a guest in a manner that suggested that he should pay his bill and enjoy himself. She still wore her long brown hair in the fashion that she had favored in the sixties—the straight, ironed look made popular by folksingers. Her pale, gray-blue eyes, hidden behind granny glasses, had browbeaten contractors and county commissioners alike. Although the Hoffmans had been in the area for ten years, they were still somewhat of a mystery to the close-knit community of Vergas, and no one knew exactly where they came from. Everybody seemed to like David, but Sharon was still referred to as "that pushy woman at the Otter Slide."

Sitting down at the office desk and mechanically putting a stack of restaurant invoices in order, David asked, "Have you given any more thought to raising Geena's salary? She is a marvelous cook, you know, and the main reason that the restaurant has been a success. We couldn't get along without her."

Sharon, reaching over David's shoulder to put the invoices back in their original order, said, "Yes, well, where else is she going to go? When Geena Olson can drive in one mile from her home and find this kind of work, I don't think we have to worry about losing her. Besides, I told her when we hired her that if it worked out we could see about a raise in a year or so. We still have four months before we really have to worry about that."

"Yes, of course, but she is working more hours and preparing more meals than either of us thought she would."

"So what? We got Sally and that other high school kid to help. Let's see how things go this summer. We'll probably have to hire even more help then."

"Well, if you say so. What do you know about this Hofstead Hail group?"

Sharon started rifling through a file folder. "Not much, really, but you might remember Myron Pekanen. He came in here a couple of nights last summer to have a few beers. He seemed to be a pretty good sort. The important thing is that this is a local conference. These people could just as well meet in their offices and go home to sleep. We've got to prove that our Winter Wonderland Weekend is of value to more than just Twin City corporations. If this is a success, we could get other bookings from groups in Fergus Falls, Alexandria, and maybe Fargo-Moorhead. And this is where you come in. You've got to keep them busy. Take them on a moonlight snowmobile safari, show them how to cross-country ski, go to the Sahlberg farm and rent that sleigh if you have to. Maybe some of them would even like to try those snowshoes you bought at that garage sale. Put a bottle of brandy in your pocket and take them for some ice fishing. I want this to be so special that it becomes an annual retreat for Hofstead Hail."

Sharon's drive and energy never ceased to amaze David. "You're wonderful, you know that? Many times over all these years I've wondered where I would be without you. Wherever that would be, I know it would not be as pleasant."

"Yes, um, thank you. Um, if we're going to make a go of this we can't sit around feeling nostalgic. Is that busboy kid here yet? What is his name again? Jeff?"

"Geoffrey. He spells his name with a 'G.' It reminds me of Geoffrey of Anjou, Henry II's father. Remember? Henry II was the guy Peter O'Toole played in both *Becket* and *The Lion in Winter?* You know, I sometimes wish I had gone back to school and finished my theater degree. I could probably have been directing plays in a college by now."

With barely disguised contempt, Sharon said, "Not bloody likely. In any event, you're not doing it now and I think I heard a car door slam. Our weekend guests are starting to arrive."

David Hoffman ambled out to the reception area just as Iris Pekanen, carrying a huge, weighty, and seemingly indestructible suitcase, pushed the door open with her ample rear end. Behind her came Pek, loaded down with the car keys. David greeted them warmly.

"Well, well, it's nice to see you again, Mr. Pekanen. And this must be your wife?"

Pek, stuffing his gloves hurriedly into his pocket to take David's outstretched hand, said, "Yah, uh, this is my wife, Iris."

Iris smiled and vigorously shook David's hand and, with a puzzled expression, said, "I didn't know you had been here before, Pek. When was that?"

Pek mumbled something incoherent about meeting a client in the restaurant but was saved from further elaboration by the arrival of the Sandbergs. As David introduced himself to the new arrivals, an air of false congeniality pervaded the room, an atmosphere that was not lightened by Clarence's astute observation of "Well, I see you made it out here, too."

Pek and Iris agreed that they had.

David brightly picked up the bags that Iris had dropped on the floor and said, "I hope you enjoy your evening with us. Mr. Hofstead suggested dinner for about six thirty. I'll show you to your rooms so you can have a chance to freshen up a bit. The bar is open, of course, so if you'd like anything, just tell me—I double as the barkeeper. Mr. and Mrs. Sandberg? If you'll just wait for me to show the Pekanens to their room, I'll be right back."

Gary Swenson and Faye Janice Nelson managed to time their arrival to coincide with that of John and Martha Hofstead. The timing, of course, had been facilitated by Gary's careful observations in his rearview mirror, proceeding at an agonizingly slow pace until he spied Hofstead's Cadillac behind them. As they came through the door, Gary was complimenting John on the brilliant idea of a Winter Wonderland Weekend. It was just what David—*maitre d'*, barkeeper, and general dogsbody—had been hoping to hear.

Gary had been priming himself for moments such as this ever since the weekend plan was announced. He prided himself on being able to read subtle hints on the faces or in the body language of other people. It was, after all, partly how he made his living as a salesman. While Hoffman was introducing himself all around and making assuring noises about the resort's amenities, however, Gary looked at his boss and found him hard to read. "Is he turning away from me slightly?" he thought. "Did he look like that when we got out of the car? Does he still resent me for not 'buying American' and driving a Saab? Sure, it's made in Sweden, but it is owned by General Motors. Was our 'coincidental' arrival transparent? Had he been talking about me to Martha? No. Martha's not giving anything away—maybe even she doesn't know who he is going to pick. But John? Hmmmm, he looks funny to me."

Flashing his most ingratiating grin, Gary said, "So, you're going to teach me to snowmobile this weekend. Hey, I really like your suit, John. That must keep you warm, huh? You know, maybe after dinner we can go for a ride. It's a marvelous night out there, but who knows how long that can last in Minnesota, right? I don't want to take a chance of missing out on snowmobiling lessons from the master."

John turned to Gary with a patient expression ("was it patient, or was it contempt?" Gary wondered) and said, "There's really nothing much to teach, you know. You just sit on the thing and twist

58

the handlebar to make it go. It's fun, though, and I think you'll like it. Um, where did that guy go off to?"

As if in answer to his question, Sharon, now wearing a wool suit designed to impress corporate America, came through the door and announced, "My husband had to attend to another matter. You must be John Hofstead. My name is Sharon Hoffman—we spoke on the telephone. Let me tell you what a privilege it is to have Hofstead Hail with us this weekend."

The rest of the introductions were made and the two couples were soon escorted to their respective rooms. As Sharon showed the Hofsteads to their room, she repeated the invitation to partake of the bar and told John that "a special selection of appetizers has been laid out just for you and your associates." Somewhat apprehensively she asked, "There is one more of your party yet to arrive. We can still expect the Kvammes, can't we?"

John Hofstead blinked as if called out of a deep hypnotic state. "Huh? Oh. Oh yes. Certainly. They should be along any time now. Remind them that we plan to eat dinner together at six thirty."

"But of course," the genial hostess replied. "Your table is all prepared."

NINE

Other than the Hofstead party, it was a quiet night at the Otter Slide Restaurant. It was already twelve degrees below zero at six o'clock, and only two other couples, determinedly celebrating their wedding anniversaries, dined that evening. Sharon thought it was just as well, in that they were understaffed to begin with and could therefore spend more time making a good impression on Hofstead Hail. Clearly, as this weekend indicated, the future was in corporate retreats.

The dinner was not the gala event that John Hofstead had envisioned. As the coffee was being served, Martha couldn't help but worry about her husband. He had intimated that he was going to use the dinner to make the big announcement on the future of the company. On the way out to the resort he had seemed his old ebullient self and seemed obviously pleased with his decision. Yet, ever since they arrived John had seemed preoccupied. A usually robust eater, he had barely eaten a third of his New York strip. Had they not been staying over for two nights, Martha would certainly have requested a doggy bag.

Because John was poor company, Martha tried her best to enjoy a pleasant conversation with Clarence. This was not easy, for Clarence had said everything interesting he ever had to say several years earlier. Nevertheless, she professed genuine interest in the fact that his Oldsmobile always started now that he had put in a tank heater, which was so much more efficient than that old head-bolt heater system.

Geoffrey, the busboy, was able to pick up snippets of conversation as he repeatedly filled the water glasses and removed plates, and had he possessed the ability to read minds, he would have heard even more.

"Did you notice how Young Gary managed to position himself so that he and Faye Janice were right next to 'Pinky'? I saw Borghild head for that chair and Gary actually slid a chair in her way so he could beat her to it."

"Get a load of that dress Iris has on. She's spilling out all over. And speaking of spilling, did her husband spend a little too much time in the bar before dinner?"

"I wish I could look like Martha. Isn't she lovely?"

"I could just kill him! I really could!"

"Psst. Get a load of Clarence. I think he's wearing the tie that he wore for his high school graduation."

"That's a lovely dress, Martha. Isn't it, Faye Janice?"

"Does dis place have cable, Borghild?"

"According to my figures, John ..."

"This is the last straw! I'm going to kill him!"

"Do they serve lo-fat ice cream here? I promised Pek that I was going to go on a diet."

"Think he's made up his mind yet? I've got to talk to him tonight."

"And I always get better gas mileage with ethanol, too."

"Well, Jane Fonda says..."

"I don't know how long I can stay with the company. It just won't be the same without John."

"Is something troubling you, dear?"

"So then Ole, he says to Lena, 'I tink we better not let our daughter go out wit dat Yohnson kid anymore.'"

"You happen to know if John is picking up the bar tab, too?"

"I've got to talk to somebody about this. This could be a real dangerous situation."

"I think it would be better if he were out of the way permanently."

"You going to eat that?"

"I've got to talk to him tonight."

"I'll see if I can get him alone sometime tonight."

"Sometimes, you just gotta act. You know, you just gotta do it."

As soon as everyone had topped off their coffee for the second time, John Hofstead rose to address the party. There didn't seem to be the usual shade of pinkness associated with him. Pallor on a pink man never looks good. There was no need to plink his spoon on the water glass, but he did it anyway.

"My good friends and associates. It is a pleasure for me to have you all together tonight. Perhaps this is something that we should have been doing more often. You know, I thought I knew you all pretty well before. But these kind of occasions, where we can all sit down together and just be ourselves, makes me realize that there's still plenty to learn about all of you, and I hope to do more of that as this weekend goes on."

Martha, who realized that John was starting to ramble, made eye contact and communicated that perhaps he should get to the point.

"Yes, well, you all know why I called you together out here."

"My God," thought Faye Janice, "that sounds like a line from an Agatha Christie play."

"And I fully expected to make an announcement at this time concerning the future of Hofstead Hail. But the more I thought about it, I decided that the best thing to do would be to talk to each of you privately. One of you, of course, will be asked to take over the company. But I want to tell each of the rest of you how much I value your contributions, how much I appreciate your service, and what I see as your role in the future of the company.

"Meanwhile," the pale pink man continued, "it's a glorious evening. Young Gary here has been telling me how much he was looking forward to a starlight snowmobile ride. Sure, it's a little cold—what? About fifteen below right now? Hey, these suits are made for that. I tell you, there's nothing more exhilarating than zooming across a frozen lake with the moon shining on the clear patches of ice." Yet, even now, in speaking about his favorite activity, Martha noticed that his enthusiasm seemed forced and artificial.

"Now, David Hoffman has assured me that all the machines are in working order. Not all of them are new, of course, but they all run. He's got a Ski-Doo, two Yamahas, a Polaris, and three Arctic Cats. Now, I've always favored the Cats, you know, ever since I bought that Arctic Cat Panther back in 1969. That little sled could go almost forty-five miles an hour on the straightaway. But tonight, I'm going to drive that new Polaris David was telling me about. Now, don't worry if you didn't bring along the right clothes. They've got everything you need right here—boots, snowmobile suits, helmets, mittens—the whole shebang. Most of it is pretty much 'one size fits all.' So, who's up for a little Minnesota Winter Wonderland?"

Young Gary immediately assented with a hearty, "Let's go!" and Faye Janice was right behind. Joey and Martha demurely excused themselves, and Harry openly scoffed and wondered, not very quietly, who would be dumb enough to go out on a frozen lake when it was fifteen below. After a hesitant soul search, Pek stood up unsteadily and announced that he was ready. Clarence, desperately hoping someone would talk him out of it and hoping that none of the boots would be his size, faked enthusiasm.

For the next two hours, the lights from snowmobiles produced an erratic but strangely hypnotic pattern on the lake. Each make of sled had a different pitch to the motor and together they produced a somewhat harmonious mechanical drone that would have disturbed any guest who was paying to sleep.

Martha knew better than to wait up for her husband when he was enjoying himself on his sleds. She thought she would turn in early. She did not hear the last snowmobile leave.

TEN

THE SITUATION AT THE Otter Slide Resort was extremely uncomfortable. The guests gradually learned of the situation of the missing Hofstead as they drifted, usually in pairs, into the restaurant
for breakfast. Clarence and Joey Sandberg were already seated in
the dining area, contented with their bowls of Malt-O-Meal, when
a distraught Martha Hofstead sought them out. No one had ever
really seen her without her public face, but this morning Mary Kay
was still in the jar. For Clarence, it was an unnerving sight.

"Have you seen John this morning ?" Martha asked nervously.

"No. Why?" replied Clarence. "Did he say he was coming in
here?"

"No," Martha said, as she joined the Sandbergs at their table.
"He didn't say anything. That is, I haven't seen him. I haven't seen
him since last night when he went snowmobiling. I don't think he
even came home last night. At first I just assumed that he had gone
to bed and that I had slept through the night without waking and
that he had gone out first thing this morning. But then I thought

that his pillow looked a little too neat, and then I noticed that his shaving kit was all zipped up, and that is so unlike John. Finally, I checked his suitcase and his pajamas were still there, all nice and fresh. John never, never goes to bed without his pajamas. Where can he be? Were you with him last night, Clarence?"

Clarence studied his coffee for a few seconds before replying. "Well, yah, for a while. But it really didn't take me too long to get my fill of snowmobiling in twenty-below weather. I was sort of hoping to get a chance to talk to him about the future of the company, but when I saw everybody take off across the lake I just gradually dropped off and came back to the resort."

"And you didn't see him come back?"

"No, I just went to our room."

"Joey? You didn't see him at all, did you?"

"I'm sorry, no, I was in our room the whole time."

With a vacant expression on his face, Clarence said, "Well, maybe he had decided who he wanted to be the next president of Hofstead Hail and spent the whole night making plans. He's probably in the resort someplace. Give him a little time."

Joey leaned over to comfort Martha and said, "Why don't you just go back to your room and get ready for the day. When I see John I'll tell him you're looking for him." She patted her on the arm with that "everything will be all right" manner.

As Martha left the room, Clarence sighed, "Well, that's that, then. If he's making plans with somebody else the handwriting is on the wall. Maybe it's just as well. I never really wanted to be a company president anyway." Morosely he made a little pit in his cereal and poured in some more cream.

Meanwhile, Iris Pekanen was doing her best to persuade her husband to rise and shine. Turning to the lump beside her in the bed she said: "You know how Hofstead values getting a good start to the day. You don't want to be the last one in for breakfast on a day like today. By the way, did you get a chance to talk to him last night?"

Hearing or seeing no evidence of a response, she tentatively shook his shoulder, "Pek? You awake?"

Pek muttered an obscenity.

"Pek? Were you drinking last night?"

Slowly Myron Pekanen opened one eye and then the other. With a maximum of effort he rotated his head a full half turn and stared maliciously at Iris. He managed to gasp, "Leave me alone."

"Pek, I'm not going to let you blow your big chance with Hofstead. Now let's get up and go to breakfast. There's a nice little coffee maker right here in the room, and I can make you a cup as you get ready. Would you like that?"

With a maximum of effort, Pekanen got himself up on one elbow and mumbled a partially sincere "Thanks."

Without further discussion, he took a therapeutic shower, put on his pants, and with a shaky hand reached for the coffee that his wife tentatively offered him. "So, did you get a chance to talk to him?"

"Who?"

"Hofstead, of course. About the job?"

"No. I didn't."

"What did you do?" Iris asked in a voice that combined dread, suffering, and reproach.

"Well, we all got dressed up in those snowmobile suits and that Hoffman guy put us on the snowmobiles, and pretty soon we were all whizzing around the lake. But everybody looks the same in those suits and I had forgotten to note what snowmobile Hofstead was on. I was chasing after one or another and I never did find the right one. It was really kind of confusing, those machines with their headlights dancing and just when you have one figured out, it changes places with the other one. Every time I caught up to one it turned out to be Young Gary. At one point I hit a drift the wrong way and tipped over. By the time I got it righted again, I was pretty much left behind. I saw the lights of Vergas across the lake and I figured I'd just go over and see if anything was going on downtown."

"And?"

"Well, I went into that bar, the one right on the corner. I was so cold by this time that I thought I'd have a little nip just to warm myself up. You know, there are some real nice people in the Vergas area. We just got to talking and I didn't feel like going out there trying to chase Pinky down. So I had a couple of drinks and then came straight back here."

"Just a couple?"

"Well, I wasn't counting."

"Perhaps you should have been."

"Oh, let's not start up again. I feel like I've been hit on the head with a hockey stick. We've got a whole weekend here. I'll have plenty of time to get my little chat with John."

"No time like the present," chirped Iris, as she flipped a brush through her hair. "Let's see if we can be the first ones down for breakfast."

Harry Kvamme scraped a chair across the floor to the breakfast table of the Sandbergs and said, "Morn—Morn! Mind if me and Borghild join you?'

There seemed to be no point in denying them permission, especially since Harry was seated before he had finished the sentence. Besides, Clarence felt uneasy about what Martha had said. Maybe Harry or Borghild knew what was going on. He waited until both were seated before he said, "By the way, either of you seen John today?"

"No," answered a disinterested Harry Kvamme, "how so?"

"Well," Joey jumped in, eager to add an air of mystery to the morning, "Martha was here just a few minutes ago looking just terrible. She said that John hadn't been in all night! She was really worried about him. Were either of you with him last night?"

"You mean," responded Borghild, in a mixture of amazement and disgust, "did we go snowmobiling? We're too old for that sort of nonsense, aren't we Harry?"

"I don't know if we're tew old," Harry chuckled, "but we're definitely tew smart."

Joey, remembering the panic in Martha's face, was becoming increasingly concerned. "So, you hadn't seen John since the supper last night?"

"No," Borghild replied. "We went back to our room, got ready for bed, and watched the news. We hadn't seen anybody else until we walked in here and saw you folks. Where do you think he went?"

Clarence nervously played with his coffee cup and said, "I think he decided who he wanted to run the company and spent all night talking to him."

Borghild looked up anxiously. "He didn't come to see us, and if he didn't come to see you, that means, well, either Pek or … oh no!"

Clarence nodded sadly, "Yup, we both know he would never pick that Finn. It's Young Gary after all."

Harry used his favorite barnyard word.

Iris and Pek entered the room just in time to hear Harry's choice expression. Iris blushed and Pek unreasonably suspected that it was directed at him. In any event, that table was full and they made their way to a separate table, muttering "good mornings" and hearing the same. As soon as they were seated, Clarence leaned back in his chair and asked them, "Have you seen John this morning?"

Pek assumed that it was Clarence's way of saying, "Has John told you I'm the new president yet?" and returned a sour and disinterested negative.

"Neither of you?"

Iris noticed an urgency in his voice. She replied, "No, why?"

"Because nobody's seen him since last night. Martha was in here a few minutes ago and was real worried. We figured he just used the time to hole up with his new president."

Pek looked up. "And that would be?"

Borghild suddenly and somewhat violently blurted out, "Well, let's put it this way: none of us!"

Iris looked around, observed who was missing, noted the resigned expressions on the faces of those present, and to everyone's surprise, repeated Harry's word. Everyone nodded.

A gloom descended on the breakfasters, a gloom that turned into hostility as Gary and Faye Janice, bright as two new pennies, energetically bounded into the room. Their hair was perfect, their teeth seemed to shine, and they were clad in matching red, white, and blue Norwegian cardigan sweaters with silver buttons.

Gary hailed his colleagues, "Hey, good morning. Good morning. Good morning all. Have a good night's sleep? We did. I tell you. Nothing like a good icy snowmobile ride to get you to gulp in that fresh air. We felt so good that we decided to forgo our usual morning jog and go cross-country skiing instead. Who's up for a little cross-country skiing this morning—after breakfast, of course?"

The invitation was met with an overwhelming lack of enthusiasm. Undeterred, Gary continued. "It isn't as bad out there as you think. I mean, there's hardly any wind. Faye Janice and I went for a little camera safari this morning. There were some deer in the woods just between the lake and the highway. I got this one shot of a buck—beautiful rack of antlers—just as the sun was rising behind him. I think it could be another prize winner."

For some reason, Gary felt that the crowd was paying more attention to him than they usually did. Finally, Clarence asked, "So, have you seen John this morning?"

As all eyes turned on him, Gary thought, "So he's made his announcement and it isn't me! You'd think he could have told me to my face!" Aloud he said, "No, I haven't seen him since last night."

Clarence persisted. "Faye Janice? Have you seen him?"

"Of course not. I've been with Gary all morning. Why? What is it?"

There was a palpable sense of relief among the rest of the breakfasters that Young Gary had not, it seemed, already been tapped as the new president of Hofstead Hail, but if Hofstead had not been with Swenson, where was he? Borghild summed up what the rest were thinking by saying, "Uffda. This could be serious."

ELEVEN

"When will I ever learn," Sheriff Palmer Knutson mumbled as he poured his second cup of French Roast coffee.

"What time was it when you finally came to bed?" asked Ellie, his wife of thirty-six years.

"A quarter to one."

"So was it worth it?"

Palmer gave her a rueful look and asked: "Is it ever? I've seen *Bride of Frankenstein* at least half a dozen times, but after the game I was too depressed to get up and go to bed. So I just started channel-surfing to see what was on. You know, the best thing about that movie is that it reminds me of the Mel Brooks version, *Young Frankenstein.*

"So the Woofies depressed you again, did they?"

"Yah, only this time it took them the whole night to do it. The game was on the West Coast, you know—the Portland Trailblazers—so it didn't start until nine thirty. Actually, you know, the Timberwolves played pretty well for most of the game. They led by five points with only twenty-seven seconds to go. Well, naturally they managed to let the Blazers tie it up and send it into overtime. A five-minute overtime! Five minutes and they ended up losing by eighteen points. How can that be possible? Can you believe it? Only the Wolves could do it. I swear, Trygve could play better than that. The Fergus Falls High School team wouldn't have lost by eighteen points in a five-minute overtime. Well, anyhow, I just couldn't summon the energy or the will to go to bed. I mean, how do you lose by eighteen points in a five-minute overtime!"

Ellie ignored Palmer's still-fuming resentment at the hapless professional athletes, none of whom he had ever met or even seen in person. "I don't think I've been able to watch television beyond midnight since Maj was born, and that's at least twenty-four years ago."

"Don't go getting old on me, Ellie."

"So staying up until almost one o'clock recaptures lost youth, huh? Go look in the mirror and tell yourself that. You look like death eating a cracker."

"I know," Palmer admitted, stifling a yawn. "I'll go to bed earlier tonight, right after *Saturday Night Live*."

"Why do you still watch that show? It hasn't been funny for years!" The conversation had been repeated in several dozen variations every winter Saturday morning over the last two decades. And for the past few years, Saturday morning had become ever more delicious. He and Ellie had celebrated their thirty-fifth wedding anniversary just last summer—a fun and sentimental celebration created by their three children. Fifteen years ago, Knutson had looked forward to going into the office on Saturday mornings because of the peace, quiet, and the absence of Saturday morning cartoons. Now, his elder daughter Maj had graduated from Gustavus Adolphus College and was in her second year of law school at the University of Minnesota. His second daughter, Amy, was a junior at Concordia College, and only Trygve remained in the nest. But Trygve, as befitting a senior in high school with a busy Friday-night schedule, rarely rose before eleven on a Saturday morning.

Palmer loved his leisurely breakfasts with Ellie. Even if they had nothing in particular to say to each other, which was rare, he loved sitting across the table from her, occasionally looking at her short, graying, light-brown hair as it spilled over her pale green eyes. She was, in truth, quite a bit plumper than the day they were married, but Palmer professed not to have noticed. This was not only politic on his part, it was also fair, for Palmer realized that he, too, had thickened in the middle. As he ate his oat bran with half a banana, he inwardly craved two scrambled eggs, hash browns, sausages, toast and jam, and a chocolate-chip cookie with his third cup of coffee. Instead, with cholesterol on his mind, he decided to smear some cream cheese on a rusk.

Palmer Knutson had been serving the citizens of Otter Tail County for thirty-six years, first as deputy and, for the last twenty years, as sheriff. Saturday mornings in January are not peak times for crime fighting, and, as the sheriff had assembled a capable team of deputies, he was able to stay away from the office more and more.

Knutson was rarely to be found in his official uniform. The last time he wore his entire uniform together was when the governor had visited Fergus Falls. He didn't like the governor, and had acted in a quite unneutral manner in helping Ellie campaign for his opponent, but the governor of Minnesota deserves respect and Palmer was finally able to find all the parts of his uniform. If he looked like a sheriff then, he certainly did not look like one now. He hunched over the breakfast table wearing a pair of doe-skin slippers, an unfashionable pair of Lee jeans, worn and faded to highlight the least attractive parts of his body, and a filthy Vikings sweatshirt. He hadn't quite gotten around to brushing either his teeth or his hair. He pushed his bifocals back into place and, unwilling and unable to further defend the folly of staying up to watch horror movies, he picked up the Minneapolis *Star Tribune* and gratefully turned to the *New York Times* crossword puzzle.

Completing the crossword puzzle on a weekday was no longer a challenge, but the Saturday puzzle, well, now, that was a challenge accepted only by the intrepid. Three minutes into the puzzle, however, the telephone rang. Desperately trying to remember a three-letter word for "table scrap," Palmer hoped the call wasn't for him. As he frantically filled in "ort," Ellie said, "It's for you, dear. Orly Peterson. Says it's important."

Having lost all concentration, Palmer gave in, tossed the newspaper aside, and picked up the telephone. "Yah, Orly. What's up? … John Hofstead? … 'Pinky'? … How long? … What was he doing out there? … Is that right? What have you done so far? … Uh-huh … Well, get anybody you can find and go out there and organize a search party. It didn't snow last night and it was pretty still, so there should be tracks to indicate if he ever left the lake. There are quite a few fish houses on that lake, aren't there? … Well, be sure you check every one of them. If he spent all night out in this cold, his chances of survival are not good. I'll come in to the office pretty soon, but don't wait for me … Yah, uh-huh … You bet. See ya."

Ellie had done the best she could to follow the conversation on Palmer's end. "Did something happen to 'Pinky' Hofstead?"

Palmer stood with the telephone receiver still in his hand. In a worried voice he replied, "Yah, he's missing. Orly's going to put together a search party. I suppose I'd better get down to the office."

"Where is he?"

Palmer peered over the top of his bifocals and said, "Well, that's the big question, isn't it?"

"No, I mean, where was he when he was last seen?"

"It seems there was some sort of company retreat up at the Otter Slide Resort near Vergas. For reasons best known to themselves they decided it would be fun to go snowmobiling. Apparently Hofstead never returned from the ride. Everybody just assumed he had quit early and had gone back to the Otter Slide. Martha didn't wait up for him, slept right through, and didn't notice that he hadn't come in until this morning."

"She just called now? She must be a sound sleeper!"

"I don't know. Orly implied that the guy who runs the place, somebody called Hoffman, had conducted his own search and fooled around much longer than he should have."

"I hope he wasn't outside last night. How cold did it get, anyway?"

"When Trygve came home last night," said Palmer, "he said it showed eighteen below on the bank sign, and that was only a little after eleven. They said on the Creature Feature that the one o'clock temperature in Fargo was 23 below. I don't think it got that cold here, but out on the lake it might have been even colder."

"Why in the world would anybody be outside snowmobiling in that kind of weather?" asked Ellie, with a mixture of awe and disgust.

"You're asking the wrong man. I've never found that kind of weather to be either fun or invigorating. A cozy furnace is a measure of man's continuing evolution. I suppose I'd better put on something that looks a little better if I'm going to go to the office."

At that moment the phone rang again and the sheriff immediately snatched at the receiver. "Yah. Hello. Knutson's . . . Ah, no . . . No . . . Oh, that's a shame . . . Who found him again? . . . Yeah, I know him. He's the mailman out there, isn't he? . . . But has it been positively identified as Hofstead? . . . Okay, well, are they sure it was an accident? . . . Well, go out there and investigate the scene. Take pictures, all the usual stuff. Then go to the Otter Slide and talk to Martha. See that relatives are notified and see that she gets home all right. Get the medical examiner to give the body a quick look, get it to the funeral home, and get everybody out of the cold."

After a long pause, during which time Ellie observed Palmer impatiently wrapping the telephone cord around his fingers and rolling his eyes, she heard, "Yah, you do that . . . No, not anymore. You can handle everything. It's your weekend on duty . . . Sure, I'll be home all day. Call anytime."

Ellie looked up anxiously. "John Hofstead?"

"Dead. Killed in a snowmobile accident. Know that big concrete loon on the shore of that lake outside of Vergas?"

"Sure. Everybody knows the Vergas loon."

"Well, it seems Hofstead got a little more intimate with it than he should have. According to the guy who found him, he drove his snowmobile right under the loon and smashed his head against its breast. The accident probably killed him, but even if it didn't, he could never have survived lying out there all night. The medical examiner can tell us, but it probably makes no difference." The sheriff sighed and added under his breath, "not to 'Pinky,' anyhow."

TWELVE

ORLY PETERSON HUNG UP the phone in his office in the Otter Tail County Law Enforcement Center and took a long-deep breath. He liked to be in charge. It had been almost a year since the sheriff had promoted him to detective, and he appreciated the increased authority that came with the job. Moreover, he felt that he had earned the confidence of his boss. They weren't really friends, and never saw each other socially, but Peterson's initial reaction, that Knutson was little more than a Norwegian country bumpkin, was obviously not true and he was in the process of gaining a great deal of respect for the man. On his part, Knutson had agonized over Peterson's promotion because he just didn't like the smarty-pants attitude of the young Swede who somehow thought a degree in criminal justice from Fergus Falls State University made him an ace crime fighter. But the sheriff was noted for his fairness, Peterson was the most qualified for the promotion, and, with a sickening knowledge that he was doing the right thing, he made Peterson his right-hand man.

It had worked out better than he could have hoped. Peterson was a computer whiz, and Knutson, who hated his own computer, could increasingly fob off all the real computer work onto his deputy. Moreover, Knutson, who used to be sort of a wunderkind of law enforcement himself, now had to admit he was getting a little long in the tooth. Orly really could relate better to the younger set, while Knutson could handle all the old people. The fact that Knutson now trusted Orly to handle the death of a prominent elderly businessman was indeed a reflection of Peterson's increased stature.

Snapping into action in his office, Peterson took the time to admire himself in his mirror and saw a reasonable facsimile of a television action-adventure star. In his view, anyone could wear a suit, but a uniform? Now that was something special! His tan uniform was spotless and pressed. The dark-brown epaulets sat easily on his broad shoulders. On the points of each collar were the gold-plated initials O.T.C.S.D., polished to pick up the Otter Tail County Sheriff's Department badge pinned over his heart and the gold five-pointed star clasp that kept his perfectly knotted brown tie in place. "Serve the people," he said, as he reached for the telephone.

In a matter of minutes the deputy had arranged for the medical examiner to accompany an ambulance to pick up the body. He also arranged for another deputy, Chuck Schultz, best known for his photography skills and for his ability to teach the D.A.R.E. program to frighten kids off drugs, to accompany him and to take photographs of the accident scene. Finally, he called the Vergas mailman who had discovered the body.

After six rings the telephone was answered with an anxious "Hello?"

"Is this the Loon's Nest Restaurant?" Orly asked.

"Yah."

"Is Arnie Holte still there? The mailman?"

"Yah, I'll get him."

After a short pause another voice answered, "Yah?"

Orly identified himself and asked, "You the guy that found the body this morning?"

"Yah."

"You identified him as John Hofstead."

"Yah."

"How can you be sure it's John Hofstead?"

"Everybody knows Hofstead. I've been buying insurance from him for thirty years."

"Right. So, who have you informed of his death?"

"You guys."

"Nobody else?"

"No, just the people in the cafe here in Vergas."

"Many people in the cafe?"

"Yah, there is. Everybody feels real bad. They all knew John Hofstead. As one of them said, 'He was the only insurance man a guy could ever trust.'"

"So who's out there with the body now?"

"I don't know. I don't think anybody is."

With a note of censure in his voice, Orly asked, "You mean you just left him out there?"

"Well, sure. Isn't that what we're supposed to do? They always say on TV that you aren't supposed to touch anything. Once I found out who it was I just came into town and reported it. There certainly wasn't anything I could do for John. He's frozen stiff as a Congressman's handshake, and I figured if I stayed out on that lake much longer I would be just like him."

"So nobody's out there?"

"Well, maybe a few people from the cafe drove out to have a look."

Orly had a vision of dozens of people milling around the accident site, playing with the body to see just how stiff it was. To Holte he said, "Look, would you mind meeting me at the site? Just go there and keep people away from the scene, would you?"

"You want me to go down there and stand around waiting for you to come from Fergus Falls? Do you know how cold it is? I'm telling you, it's a bad day for brass monkeys, if you know what I mean."

Orly acknowledged the crude, but totally apt metaphor, and said, "You don't have to stand outside. Just wait in your car. And if anyone comes, just tell them to keep away until we get there. It won't be that long. Now, you say it happened by that big loon?"

"Yah, from what I seen, it looked like he just got under it a little too far and he hit his head and that's all it took."

"All right, we'll be right out. And Arnie?"

"Yah?"

"We really do appreciate this, you know."

"Yah, you bet."

Orly and Deputy Schultz picked up Dr. Jimmy Clark at his residence on Beech Avenue and, followed by an ambulance, proceeded to the scene of the accident. In spite of his youthful name, Jimmy

Clark was sixty-six years old and looked every year of it. He was something of a government double-dipper in that in addition to his regular position at the state hospital, he had been the Otter Tail County medical examiner for the last twenty years. A little man swaddled in a down parka and a fur hat, he entertained Orly all the way to Vergas with his stories of cold-weather deaths he had known. It took at least forty minutes to get to Vergas in the wintertime, a fact well known by Arnie Holte, who had decided there was really no reason not to finish his second cup of coffee. He still had plenty of time to shoo away gapers and to get cold by the time Orly and Dr. Clark got there.

Arriving in Vergas, the two-vehicle procession passed through the block-long business district and drove east of town on Highway 228. Orly began to think about loons. The Vergas loon, a masterpiece of kitsch, is not as old, nor as frequently photographed as some of Minnesota's other notable statues. Paul Bunyan and Babe grace the lake in Bemidji and claim to be America's second-most-photographed statues+- (presumably trailing only the Statue of Liberty), but the Vergas loon is thirty years younger and has a lot of catching up to do. Likewise, although it is taller and constructed out of more permanent concrete, it is off the beaten track of motorists who may be more familiar with the fiberglass prairie chicken of Rothsay. The loon of Vergas stands about twenty feet high in a special park overlooking beautiful Long Lake. In the summer the park features a sandy beach, a changing house, a fishing pier, a swimming dock, and a water slide. The big loon seems to gaze out over the lake in a paternalistic manner to defend the rights and liberties of more normal-sized loons. Both birds, feathered and concrete, are magnificent. As the state bird of Minnesota, the loon embodies all the things Minnesotans like to believe about themselves. They are loyal (they mate for life), they care about their young (Minnesota always ranks at the top in education), and they are majestic and beautiful (all fifty states—some without merit—make this claim). But there is something very special about being at a Minnesota lake in the summer, when it finally gets dark, to hear the weird and forlorn call of a loon.

Orly had tuned out Clark's cold-weather stories and was now reminiscing about how he had parked down by the loon with "um, what was her name? She was that tall girl who went to St. Cloud State and she…"

Clark jabbed Orly in the ribs and giggled, "So they just decided to bury him the way he was. Nobody cared back in those days. Hey, that must be the mailman you put in charge. He's waving you over to the driveway."

In fact, the driveway down to the park was not cleared of snow and there was barely room for three cars to park on the edge of the road. As they climbed out of the car, Orly could tell that Holte had done an acceptable job of keeping people from the scene. Only one pair of footprints, presumably his, led down to the prone figure at the base of the concrete loon. In the back seat, Deputy Schultz got out his camera, rolled down the window, and said, "How about if I just take the pictures from here? It's so cold out that the camera is going to freeze up anyway and this gives a nice distant shot."

"Sure, take one from here," Peterson snapped. He did enjoy ordering lesser ranks around. "But then you get down there with us and you take pictures of everything. Stay away from the body and stay out of the tracks until you get everything photographed. Just keep the camera inside your coat until you're ready to shoot."

The deputy did as he was told, muttering out of earshot what he thought of Orly Peterson and his fanatic attention to detail and routine. Meanwhile, Orly surveyed the scene. It looked simple enough. Hofstead's snowmobile had come off the lake on a big drift that carried it onto the shoreline. He had avoided the trees and apparently had meant to just drive by the loon. From the evidence of the snowmobile tracks, however, it appeared that he had failed to notice that the loon sat on a small concrete pedestal. One of the skis had clearly hit the pedestal and this would have caused the snowmobile to rise up suddenly just as the driver passed under the loon. It seemed obvious that John Hofstead, as accomplished a snowmobiler as he was, had bounced up and hit his head and had fallen from the sled, which had continued to run until it had reached the lake again. Whether he had died from the force of hitting his head against the concrete loon or whether he had been knocked unconscious, never to wake up in the sub-zero weather, was yet to be determined.

It had not snowed since the accident and the tracks of the snowmobile were clear. So, too, were the tracks made by Arnie Holte when he had discovered the body.

There were no other tracks leading from the loon to the lake or from the loon to the highway. Fifty feet beyond the loon, on the clear ice of Long Lake, rested the sleek new Polaris that had given "Pinky" Hofstead his last ride.

"Make sure you get a picture of that Polaris down there, and take a picture of the right front ski to see if it got splintered on that cement thing the loon is sitting on," ordered the authoritarian Peterson. "Jimmy? What do you need to do here?"

"Nothing," said the medical examiner, his mouth twisted in an expression of distaste. "I'm freezing my patoot off. Let's get him in the ambulance and get out of here."

With that, he waved the ambulance attendant over, and in a short time Hofstead was at last ready to conclude his Winter Wonderland Weekend. "Jimmy, why don't you go on back with the ambulance. I'll go on over to the Otter Slide and break the news to Mrs. Hofstead. They're probably still searching for poor Pinky, unless somebody from the Loon's Nest has gone over to tell them about it." Squaring his shoulders and opening the door, Orly said, "Come on, Chuck—this is the part of the job nobody likes."

THIRTEEN

ORLY PETERSON AND CHUCK Schultz were shown into that part of the Hoffman living quarters that doubled as the resort office. Ever since he had met them at the door, David Hoffman had subjected them to a barrage of self-justification about how he couldn't be expected to look after all of his guests, that it wasn't his fault if a man didn't tell his wife where he was going, and after all, when a man goes out on a new Polaris snowmobile, there's no telling how far he's going to go, but that it was such a fine new machine and that once he noted that it was missing he was sure that Hofstead— who was a snowmobiling fanatic after all, I mean, you'd have to be to go out in that cold last night, wouldn't you?—had just gone out for more snowmobiling and that he was sorry he had to call them up on such a little thing but the man's wife was worried and insisted on it, and what's a man to do? I mean the customer has to be served, and would they like to sit down?

Orly was somewhat dazed by this volcano of words and was determined not to lose his meager opening. "Yes, that will be fine, but" he almost shouted, "first I'm afraid I have some bad news for you."

The nervous jabbering of Hoffman rapidly subsided into a worried gasping sound. "Yes? Yes? What is it? Have you found Hofstead?"

"I'm afraid John Hofstead has met with an accident. He's dead. I'll need to inform Mrs. Hofstead, and then I'd like to talk to you, if I may. Would you be so kind as to bring Mrs. Hofstead here?" As Hoffman stood there with his mouth hanging open, Orly added, "Now?"

Orly had never spoken to Martha Hofstead, but he knew who she was. Martha, for her part, had only to recognize the uniform to realize that this was not a routine visit. She had been hoping that she was being called in to aid with the search for her husband, but one look at the young and inexperienced deputy's face told her that he was the bearer of bad news. The other deputy, Chuck Schultz, politely mumbled when he was introduced to her and quickly returned his gaze to his feet. Nevertheless, it was still a shock to her when Orly said, "Mrs. Hofstead, I'm afraid I have some very bad news for you. Would you please sit down?"

Martha did as she was told.

"This morning, about an hour ago," continued Orly Peterson, nervously consulting his watch, "your husband was found underneath the loon at the end of the lake. It appears he was driving his snowmobile near the statue, came too near it, and bumped his head and fell. He was dead at the scene."

At the word "dead" Martha let out an involuntary gasp.

"I have just come from the scene of the accident. Jimmy Clark, our medical examiner, accompanied me and we have taken the body … er … your husband to the, uh, morgue. On your instructions, we will notify the funeral home of your choice to, uh, you know, take it, uh, him from there."

Martha was whimpering softly and Orly somewhat awkwardly put his arm around her. "Please, Mrs. Hofstead, if there is anything we can do, just let us know. Are there any relatives that you would like us to notify? Is there anyone special that you would like to have with you at this time?"

Martha sobbed, "Yes. I want Borghild. Can I see Borghild?"

Peterson made a stiff but perceptible nod to David Hoffman, who went scurrying after Borghild Kvamme. As Martha wept and Schultz continued to stare at the floor, Orly Peterson breathed deeply and thought, "yah, this is part of the job, too. And I don't think I'll ever be any good at it."

Borghild entered the room and wordlessly helped Martha to her feet. She held her in her arms for several minutes as Martha's body convulsed with sobs. Finally, she said, "Come on, let's go back to your room," and led her meekly away.

After an embarrassed silence, Orly said, "And now, Mr. Hoffman, if I may have a few words with you?"

For the briefest of seconds, Hoffman had the look of a scared rabbit. Then he abruptly said, "Let me go get my wife."

As Hoffman left the room, Deputy Schultz said, "What you wanna talk to them for? The guy's dead; we told the widow. Let's go back to town."

"Now look, Chuck. You know how Palmer likes to have everything done right and all bases covered. He put me in charge and I don't want him to give me any of that 'How come you didn't do such-and-such?' stuff. These people are the owners of the resort and the owners of the snowmobile that killed a guy. So maybe there's a wrongful death suit. Ever think of that? So we go to court and some hotshot lawyer asks, 'What does the sheriff's report say?' You gotta think of those things. I had this one professor in a criminal justice class that kept saying, 'Get down all the facts. You can decide later what's relevant.'"

Chuck Schultz, who had not attended college, had no intention of doing so, and tended to resent anyone who had, was not impressed. "Like, all right, so, he goes, 'Yah, I saw him go out on a snowmobile. I didn't see him come back.' And we go, 'Thanks for your extremely valuable cooperation!' That it?"

Orly had never had much success in enlightening Schultz on the finer points of serving the law and the citizen. Now he merely looked pugnaciously at Schultz and said, "Yah, that's about it."

At that moment, Hoffman returned and introduced his wife to Peterson and Schultz. Orly was not prepared for meeting Sharon Hoffman. Whereas the husband had been a meek, soft-spoken, chubby little fellow, Orly was taken aback by the force of Sharon's domineering manner. Her voice, even in the fatuous "How do you do?" was of such a quality that Orly began to feel he should apologize for his presence. She was at least three inches taller than her husband, and her pale blue eyes seemed to say, "Let's get this over with. I'm a busy woman." Somewhat flustered, Orly shook her huge hand and said, "If we could just trouble you for a few minutes, uh, for our report, you know."

"Of course. What would you like to know? Has David offered you any coffee?"

"Well, uh, ah ..."

"He didn't? David! For heaven's sake, get these men some coffee."

As David quietly disappeared in the direction of the kitchen, Orly leaned back and decided that the impending coffee demanded an informal approach. "So, you've got a nice place here. How long have you been running it?"

"We'll be starting our eleventh year this May."

"But," Orly asked, "this hasn't always been open in the winter has it?"

"No, this is our first year as an all-weather resort."

"How's it going?"

"Can't complain. Or at least, it wouldn't do us any good if we did, would it? No, we won't quite break even by keeping it open this winter. But we didn't really expect to our first year. Next year will be the real test. We've had enough interest so that I think next year could be a real breakthrough."

"Yah, well, winter sports are getting to be real popular. Especially now that they got lightweight clothes so you can get out and enjoy things. I've even been out to Andes Towers Hills over by Alexandria a few times." Orly smiled as he thought of the shapely form of his girlfriend, Allysha, in a ski outfit.

"Well, that's what we thought. We don't have a high enough hill around here for a downhill run, but there are plenty of beautiful cross-country ski areas. Maplewood State Park isn't that far away. And, of course, snowmobiling has always been popular."

"Are you into snowmobiling yourself?" Orly asked, mainly to keep the conversation going until the coffee arrived.

"Yes," Sharon smiled, pushing her long brown hair away from her eyes. "About five years ago we bought a big old Arctic Cat

440 Puma at an auction sale. It's almost like an antique now, of course, and we don't have it for our guests to ride. But that got us started. David, you know, had never really had a hobby, and he really started to get interested in snowmobile racing." She lowered her voice, "Frankly, I think he finally found one avenue for unsuspected aggression and competitiveness. Anyway, pretty soon he was zooming around those oval tracks, competing in lake enduros, and having the time of his life." As David came in with the coffee, she continued, "Weren't you, dear?"

"Weren't I, er, wasn't I what?"

"Enjoying your snowmobiles."

"Oh, yes, certainly," Hoffman said. He was immediately so distracted that he sat down with the coffee pot in his hands as Chuck forlornly held out his empty cup. "We are quite the snowmobilers, you know. Why, I even competed in the International 500 race."

Chuck burst in, "You did? Hey, that was the big one. The one from Thunder Bay to St. Paul. How did you do?"

David smiled modestly, "Well, I didn't win. But I didn't expect to. I just entered for the experience. What matters to me is that I finished! Most people can't say that. It's quite a ride. You twist and turn and run into rocks and trees. There isn't a spot ten feet long that's smooth. And it's really, really tough on the body." Impatiently Sharon spun her index finger around to indicate that he should finish serving the coffee.

"Gotta be in pretty good shape, huh?" asked Chuck.

"David may not look like an athlete," Sharon unexpectedly put in, "but he takes good care of himself. Don't you, dear?"

Deftly fielding what he considered to be a compliment, David continued. "Actually, the year I finished was the second time I entered the International. The first time I broke a sway bar right about at the Canadian border. This caused the steering to lock and it really slowed me down. I quit when I got to Duluth. But the second time? That was something! There were about three hundred and fifty contestants in all. And you could tell almost from the start who would finish, you know, the ones who had double welds on their machines and who had changed shocks and put on skid plates. And not all of them made it either. At one point the whole race was stopped after several sleds collided in the woods. They had to get medical helicopters to fly in and take people away to the hospital. But I made it all the way."

Chuck nodded in appreciation. "All the way to St. Paul, huh?"

"Well, technically no. But all the way to Forest Lake, where the race ended. That was good enough for me," David added.

Orly thought he had done enough in the way of paying for his coffee with polite conversation and was eager to proceed with the matter at hand. Turning back to Sharon, he asked, "And so, you now have snowmobiles available for your guests to use?"

"Yes, we have six sleds."

Mentally totaling up the cost of snowmobiles, Orly raised his eyebrows and said, "That represents quite an investment."

Sharon, pleased that another man had been impressed with her capital investments, said, "Well it does, of course, but only one of them is new. We bought a new Polaris this year, and the dealer let us buy some additional used ones. You see, we had two Arctic Cat sleds before—the big ones, a ZR-580 and a ZR-440. Those things can hit speeds of up to a hundred miles an hour, you know. Well, we didn't want our guests driving anything like that, and we had modified them for racing on ice by putting metal studs in the track and by adding these sharp carbide skegs to the skis. I mean, they were really beautiful machines—I won a few races on ice myself—but probably not the most practical sleds for anything but racing. So, we got the dealer to take them in trade and we came back with one new Polaris and a motley collection of Yamahas, Ski-Doos, and one little Arctic Cat."

"And last night? Were they all in use?"

"David? Were all the sleds in use last night?"

"Yes," replied the mild innkeeper. "I thought that perhaps all the couples would each go two to a sled. But it didn't work out that way. Everyone wanted their own."

"And who would that be," Orly continued.

"Let's see." Hoffman scowled. "There was Mr. Hofstead. He said his wife wouldn't be coming and he wanted the new Polaris. I figured since it was his party, that was only right. Then there was Mr. Pekanen. He had a Ski-Doo. And Mr. Sandberg, he had the other Ski-Doo. Then there was the Swenson-Nelson couple. I thought they could go together, but then they saw those matching Yamahas and decided that they each had to have one. Those are nice sleds—Exiter II STs—mountain sleds, you know—570cc liquid cooled twin and Mikuni carbs! And, well, I guess that's about it."

"But didn't you say that all six sleds were being used last night?"

"Huh?"

"That's only five."

"Oh, of course. I drove the other one, the Cat, myself. I wasn't sure I trusted those people to drive around on a cold night all by themselves, especially Pekanen and Sandberg, who acted like they had never been on a machine before. In fact, the only one I had complete confidence in was Hofstead, and he was the one who had the accident. Isn't that ironic?"

"Um, yes it is," Orly agreed. "Now, you all went roaring off across the lake. Who was in the lead?"

David looked surprised that the questions should have been asked. "I was, of course."

"The whole time?"

Hoffman leaned forward to refill Orly's coffee cup before replying. "No, come to think of it, just at the beginning. It seemed that as the guests got a little more confident in handling their machines, they started to be a little more daring. They would surge ahead or go off the track for a ways. But we stayed together for quite a while. By then, I was more confident that they could handle their sleds and I paid less attention."

"Well, somehow, Mr. Hofstead must have gotten separated from the group. Wouldn't you have noticed that?"

"No, no. It wasn't like that. When you are out in front of a group of snowmobilers you don't always look back to take roll call. You just go. At one point I noticed one sled turn and go back in the direction of the Otter Slide. After a while I noticed that there were only four of us out there so I figured another one must have gone back."

"Couldn't you tell who had gone back and who was still with you?"

"No. Not at night. If it had been day I could have been able to at least tell you what kind of sled it was. In fact, if I hadn't been driving a sled myself, I could have told you what kind of sled it was just by the sound. But it was dark. And I couldn't hear anything above the noise of my own machine. All you can really see out there are the lights, and that could have come from anyone. In fact, there are a lot of people in Vergas who own sleds. It could have been anybody from around here."

"So when you came home, did the rest follow?"

"At that point there were three machines zipping back and forth on the clear portion of the ice. They were racing and having a good time and so I just waved to one of them—I have no idea who it was, maybe he didn't even see me—and I came back to the resort. We work long hours here, you know, and I was pooped."

"And none of them followed you back?"

"To tell you the truth, I didn't look to see. I just parked my sled and came in and went to bed. I didn't know Mr. Hofstead hadn't come back until this morning."

"So it's entirely possible that Mr. Hofstead could go off by himself and no one would have noticed?"

"That's right," Hoffman said, and massaged the sides of his face with both hands. "I feel just terrible about it. But we can't keep our eyes on all our guests all of the time. He was an experienced snowmobiler. I just can't believe he could have had such a misfortune. Still, I guess it happens to everyone. When your ticket number is called, you gotta answer, right?" His wife stared at him as though she expected him to admit liability at any moment.

"What?" asked Chuck Schultz. "Answer what number?"

"Thank you, Mr. Hoffman," Orly cut in. "We won't take any more of your time. I'm sorry about this and appreciate your cooperation. I hope that other 'Winter Wonderland Weekends'—that what you call 'em?—will be more successful. Mrs. Hoffman? Nice to meet you and thank you for the coffee. Let's get back to town, Chuck."

The news of the death of John Hofstead rapidly spread among the guests of the Otter Slide Resort. Borghild and Harry agreed to take Martha back to Fergus Falls. Gary Swenson volunteered to drive Hofstead's car back to town, but unfortunately so did Clarence Sandberg and Myron Pekanen. What was becoming an ugly and uncomfortable scene was ended when Chuck Schultz appeared and said, "I'm supposed to drive Hofstead's car back to town. Who's got the keys?"

Within thirty minutes David and Sharon were alone at the Otter Slide. An irregular and tragic parade made its way back to Fergus Falls. Inside their cars, the participants of the Winter Wonderland Weekend were alone with their grief and alone with the question: "How does this affect my place in Hofstead Hail?"

FOURTEEN

It was Tuesday morning at 6:40 am. The clock radio on the nightstand next to the sleeping head of Palmer Knutson came on to the sounds of "He knows all, he tells only some. He's Mr. Sports, Mr. Action, Mr. Jim Ed Poole." The sheriff opened his eyes, and he faced what he hoped would be the two most difficult tasks of the day. First—a job that was getting harder every day—he had to amputate his body from his bed and face a day that as yet had shown no promise of a sun. In January, the sun seldom rose before eight o'clock, and Knutson saw no reason why he should either. But he did so because of the second most difficult task of the day. He and Ellie had to get their son, Trygve, off to school.

As he lay in bed listening to the Morning Show and the unenthusiastic report on the Super Bowl as given by Minnesota Public Radio's finest, two thoughts mingled. He detested fate and the usual cheating referee decisions that had deprived the Vikings of a spot in the Super Bowl, and he looked forward to next year, when the Eaglet would be out of the nest, off to college, and he wouldn't have to get up before he felt like it. Usually, he felt like getting up at 7:15. It was only thirty-five minutes later, but it was a time of his choosing. His failure to overcome his nocturnal inertia enabled Ellie to beat him into the shower. He was glad.

"Bad business with poor old Pinky Hofstead," he thought, "but Orly handled everything all right. The more he lightens up on the Ace Crime Fighter bit and does more things like that, the better deputy he will become." He breathed deeply, cracked his knuckles and several other joints, and accepted the inevitable.

At least, Palmer and Ellie no longer had to worry about Trygve catching the bus. His clever arguments had convinced his parents that the most logical solution to the family's transportation crisis was to purchase another car. Trygve often went to school early for academic events, and stayed after school for athletic events. By letting him have a car, it solved everybody's scheduling problems. Palmer and Ellie had rather favored a brown Plymouth Reliant, but they agreed to let Trygve help in the selection. Now Palmer himself felt a little self-conscious hopping into a bright orange Pontiac Firebird. But, on the other hand, he remembered what it was like to be young, and as long as the kid kept his grades up, well …

Palmer and Ellie never really got around to having their own breakfast until Trygve was pushed out the door. At last this was accomplished, and they sat with the newspaper and some raisin bagels smothered in what Palmer realized was far too much butter. After a comfortable silence, Palmer said, "You know, I think I maybe ought to go to John Hofstead's funeral."

Ellie, who was still wrapped in her bathrobe, said, "Are you thinking we both should go? We didn't really know them that well. I mean, we go to the same church and all that, but they always went to the early services and we went to the late one. Our paths have hardly crossed."

"Yah," Palmer acknowledged with a curious intake of breath, "but he was a good man. And Martha always seemed like such a nice person."

"I suppose there will be a full church. He had a lot of friends."

"Yah, if you don't go it almost looks like you weren't one of his friends."

"Well, were you?"

"Sure, sort of."

Ellie's eyes twinkled as she added, "And it never hurts for an elected official to appear before a large crowd, right?"

"Hey. Is that fair? I think it would be a nice gesture of respect. Besides, I want to hear what Rolf will say. He always comes through for big funerals."

"Rolf" referred to the Reverend Rolf Knutson, Palmer's older brother, the senior pastor of the First Norwegian Lutheran Church. Whenever he and his brother stood nose to nose, Palmer was shocked to discover that they were of the same height. Rev. Knutson had silver hair, large silver eyebrows, and a silver voice. In his majestic robes he seemed larger than life. Palmer, the kid brother, had always been in awe of him.

Rather than going to the office, coming home to change into a nice funeral suit, and then change again, Palmer decided to "catch up on some paper work at home," as he referred to a leisurely perusal of the newspaper. He called the law enforcement office and left word that he would be in the office shortly after the funeral.

The weather had moderated, he noticed, as he drove his Acura Integra to the funeral. It was at last above zero, the first time in five days, and mourners could get by with overcoats instead of fur-lined parkas. As he had anticipated, the church was packed. There were insurance colleagues from all over the state. There were local service club contingents and the new president of Fergus Falls State University. The president of Concordia College, the beneficiary of the Hofstead largess, had also made the sixty-mile drive to attend.

The Reverend Knutson was at his best, linking the deceased's career in insurance "to that insurance which Christ has provided for our salvation." There were never very many negative things that could have been said about John Hofstead in the first place, and whatever they were, they were certainly not mentioned on this day. When Reverend Knutson spoke, it was assumed God listened and people were assured by the Lutheran conclusion: "Into your hands, O merciful Savior, we commend your servant, John Hofstead. Acknowledge, we humbly beseech you, a sheep of your own fold, a lamb of your own flock, a sinner of your own redeeming. Receive him into the arms of your mercy, into the blessed rest of everlasting peace, and into the glorious company of the saints in light. Amen."

A pleasant lunch followed.

That afternoon snow began to fall. The mourning, for all but the closest family members of John Hofstead, was over. The whiteness settled down over the First Norwegian Lutheran Church and over the beautiful Otter Tail County Court House. It partially obscured the Fergus Falls State Hospital, on the hill overlooking the town. It covered up dirt and soot and grime as perfectly as the Reverend Knutson had maintained that God's forgiveness covered the sins of mankind. It looked so pure that the sheriff could not bring himself to pore over crime statistics or worry about problems in less blessed places. Instead, since the life of the late John Hofstead was fresh in his mind, he decided to wrap up things and asked Orly Peterson to bring in the file.

As Orly came in he was chuckling, and before Palmer could stop him he said, "So Ole, he decided he was going to be Norway's first astronaut, see, and he proudly told Sven that he was going to be the first man on the sun. Well, Sven, he looks at him for a few seconds and says, 'Don't be silly, Ole. You can't go to the sun, you'd burn up!' But Ole says, 'No, no, I got dat figured out. I'll go at night.'"

Palmer's facial muscles moved less than those of a dead walleye as he took the folder out of his deputy's hand. "Is everything you told me, and all your notes, in this folder?"

"Yah," Orly said, the smile fading into an equally fish-like solemnity.

"And there's nothing new to add to it?"

"Not that I can think of. I got the pictures of the scene of the accident developed. I put them in."

"But basically, I can feel safe about skimming this report and not waste too much time on it?"

Orly shrugged so that his epaulets flapped. "I think so."

The sheriff began to scan the pages of the report. "You know, you've gotten to be a much better writer in the last couple of years. Detail. I like your detail . . . Yah, good report. And this is where it happened. Right under the loon?"

"Yah, I'm afraid so. It's almost the sort of thing that could appear in that News of the Weird. 'Man Killed By Twenty-Foot Loon.' Although it wasn't very funny at the time, only cold. But you can see how it must have been for the poor guy. Bam! He hits the statue and that's all she wrote. Notice how pure and even the snow is? He just laid there until we came. The only footprints you can see there are ours."

Palmer Knutson studied the picture for a long time. Finally, he asked, "Where's the snowmobile?"

"Well, Chuck couldn't get that in the picture. It's about fifty feet away, down on the lake."

"Did he take a picture of that, too?"

"Of course. He wasn't too enthusiastic, but I made him do it. It's right at the back of the report. You can even see how the exhaust of the snowmobile engine had discolored the area right around it. Those things do cause pollution, you know. I figured it coasted down to the lake and the engine kept running until it ran out of gas."

"I notice that the track of the snowmobile shows that it went exactly between two small trees to get down to the lake. Could you see any other tracks around the snowmobile?"

"Of course not. Hofstead had fallen off by that time. Besides, it had coasted just to the edge of the clear ice. That stuff wouldn't take tracks."

Palmer Knutson looked out the window. "It might have, you know, but they are covered now." He added, after a long pause, "That's too bad, it might have told us something. And you're sure that the snowmobile was at least fifty feet from Hofstead's body?"

"Yah, at least. How come? What's the big deal?"

A knot had grown in the sheriff's stomach. He looked up at his deputy, back at the picture, and then back at Orly. Finally, in a husky whisper, he said, "The big deal is, I'm afraid, that John Hofstead was murdered."

FIFTEEN

ORLY AND CHUCK SCHULTZ rode in silence in the white Sheriff Department's Ford Bronco. They were towing an empty snow-mobile trailer up Highway 59 on the way to the Otter Slide. Orly hadn't relished the thought of another assignment with Schultz, but he was on duty, and at least he was familiar with the basic outlines of the case. The basic outlines, however, were all that Orly was planning to give him, at least for the present.

Chuck, who was driving, casually removed both hands from the wheel to make the universal "how come" sign. "So how come we gotta go all the way to Vergas to pick up this snowmobile? It wasn't stolen, was it?"

"Geez, look out, Chuck, this highway's icy. No, nobody thinks it was stolen, the sheriff just wants to take a look at it, that's all."

"Is it the snowmobile that guy was riding on who got himself killed?"

"Yah."

"Oh, I see. In case there's some lawsuit against the resort, they figure they better examine it for flaws, poor maintenance, liability, stuff like that there."

Orly, realizing that he would not have to labor to keep Chuck in the dark, said, "Yah, essentially, that's it. The sheriff just wants somebody to look at it."

This seemed to satisfy Chuck, who, oblivious to an oncoming truck filled with frozen turkeys, leaned forward to fiddle with the radio dial to tune in one of his favorite country music stations.

Orly winced and mentally tuned out. He turned his mind back to his conversation with Palmer Knutson. When the sheriff had first mentioned the word "murdered," Orly thought he had said that John Hofstead was "murmured." It made no sense, and after a full ten seconds, he said, "Huh?"

"I said," repeated the sheriff, more loudly and distinctly, "that I think it is a very good possibility that John Hofstead was murdered."

"But how? And why? Who would want to kill a guy like John Hofstead? I mean, what makes you say that? There's nothing in my report that could remotely suggest that."

"No, no there isn't. And I'm not criticizing your report. It's a good report. In fact, it is your report and your pictures that make me question the death."

Flattered, but still curious, Orly blurted out, "So what is it?"

"Look," the sheriff began, spreading out the photographs, "you have reported that you found a single snowmobile track going up to and under the loon and that the track is unbroken until it gets to the lake. Right?"

"Right."

"These tracks were clear? There had been no wind to erase them?"

"No. I mean, yes, they were clear and no, there hadn't been any wind to erase them."

"Okay. Now, when you ride a bike and fall off, the bike rolls down the hill, doesn't it?"

"Yah, unless it falls over."

"All right. And a snowmobile doesn't fall over very often. It's like a car in that respect. So what would happen if a guy fell out of a car when it's in gear?"

"Well, I suppose the car would keep going, at least until it ran into something."

"Right again. But how is a snowmobile different from a car? Other than being considerably colder, of course."

"What do you mean?"

"How do you make it go?"

Orly stood and then went into a half crouch, his hands extended as though they were holding a snowmobile. "Well, you sit on it and twist that rubber end on the handlebar—the same as you do with a motorcycle."

"So, you see what I'm getting at?"

"Not really," Orly replied, showing traces of annoyance. "Look, do we have to play 'Encyclopedia Brown' with this question?"

"Okay," the sheriff allowed, realizing that he was beginning to sound supercilious. "With a motorcycle, the wheels would run down the hill over the bare ground to the lake. But a snowmobile runs on a broad track and it runs on snow. When the hand is removed from the accelerator, the machine stops, and it stops in a hurry when it is on about six inches of soft snow. Now. Look at your report and look at that picture."

"Ah."

"Exactly! How did that machine get all the way down to the lake? That's a good fifty feet! In soft snow!"

Orly leaned over and pointed at the picture. "But there couldn't have been anyone else there. I would have noticed their footprints. Look for yourself. There is not a footprint anywhere near the body in those first photographs, and none whatsoever by the snowmobile. Who do you think committed a murder, the loon? Some evil spirit that exists to animate a twenty-foot concrete bird to kill elderly insurance salesmen? Or maybe someone drove by on the highway and with a precise remote-controlled toy helicopter steered the snowmobile into the loon and then undertook to guide it down to the lake. Perhaps it was an elaborate case of suicide and Hofstead did himself in after staging a way for the sled to keep going just long enough so it would look like an accident and so there wouldn't be any problem collecting life insurance from his own company. Or maybe he was unsatisfied with the accommodations at the Otter Slide so he decided to make trouble for that poor sap who runs the place by getting himself killed just to give the place a bad name. I can't explain how that snowmobile got down to the lake, but murder? I think not!"

"Orly, Orly, Orly. The explanation is as simple as pie. But you may be right. Maybe it wasn't murder. I sure hope it wasn't. But we have to look into this, it is just too big an anomaly to ignore. Maybe something mechanical could go wrong with the snowmobile. Maybe it just got stuck. We have to find out, in any event. Here's what I want you to do. Take somebody with you and bring back that snowmobile so we can have it examined. You were up there before and you know the people. And for God's sake, don't say, 'We gotta check this out because the sheriff thinks it was murder.' I'm not even very sure I do, although I have a real nasty feeling about it. Don't tell anybody about this, including whoever you take with you up to Vergas. Just tell those resort people—what were their names, the Hoffmans?—that we merely want to cover all bases in case anyone should question the safety of the snowmobile—the manufacturer, the retailer, whatever. Maybe it is all my imagination, but Orly, this could have been murder, and it could have been a relatively easy murder."

Orly had seen Knutson in one of these all-knowing poses before, and it drove him nuts. "Are you going to sit there and play the inscrutable Charlie Chan or are you going to tell me how it could have been done?"

"No, no I'm not. Not right now. I'm going to see what we can get from a mechanic on that snowmobile. That way, if it were just an accident, I can tell you about my theory and you can tease me about being wrong and no harm done. Meanwhile, try to figure it out for yourself. I'll say one more thing about it, however, and that is if I'm right, we won't have to go far to find a narrow range of suspects. You think about it!"

Orly thought about it, and continued to do so as he noted that Chuck Schultz totally ignored the speed limit as he passed through the village of Elizabeth. When no easy answer was forthcoming, he also thought about how he would like to add to the Otter Tail County murder total the name of one sheriff.

The snow continued to fall and the traffic was light on the other side of Pelican Rapids. Orly was still trying to see how "easy" it would have been to commit a murder without leaving tracks when Chuck interrupted his reverie. "You know, it'll be after dark by the time we get that snowmobile loaded. If we don't hurry too much, we should be able to stop in Pelican on the way back and have supper and charge it to the department. What d'ya say?"

Orly generally selected his dining companions with great care, a care which would have precluded Chuck Schultz. But under the circumstances, thinking about a lonely dark apartment with no food versus a free meal, he saw the advantage of Chuck's suggestion. After all, the sheriff hadn't imparted any sense of urgency. Who cared when they got the snowmobile back in town. "Yah," Orly agreed. "Why not?" This cheered Chuck up to the extent that he didn't even complain when Orly leaned over to switch the radio to "All Things Considered."

David Hoffman was waiting for them in the reception area. Orly noted that he seemed agitated and overly anxious to please. This time he had a coffee pot and cups all ready for them. Orly was prepared to decline, but Chuck walked past him, sat down, poured a cup, leaned back, smacked his lips, and let out a contented "Ah." Orly then remembered Chuck's determination to delay their return until they could collect on a county meal. It was just as well, for Orly had decided to collect just a little more preliminary information from Hoffman on the off chance that a murder had been committed. In any event, it would seem a nice chat was required to soothe the visibly jumpy Hoffman.

"Now, I've got everything all ready, I think," Hoffman said. "I was so surprised when the sheriff called. I did everything you told me to do at the time. I drove the snowmobile back here after you left on Saturday. As you had surmised, it had run out of gas. I had Sharon take me out there on another sled, and I brought along gas so I could drive it home. I haven't started it since or touched it in any way. As I told the sheriff, I just parked it in the shed when I got home and haven't touched it since. I haven't even touched it since."

Orly, with tongue in cheek, asked, "So you haven't touched it since?"

"No, I haven't touched it since. This seemed to be important to the sheriff and so I told him I hadn't touched it since I brought it in. I'm still not clear, however, just why you want to examine it. The sheriff seemed rather evasive about it."

"Oh, no," Orly reassured him. "He didn't mean to be evasive. You know Sheriff Knutson. He's on top of things. What would happen if the family of John Hofstead were to sue the Polaris corporation for wrongful death? They'd want to have all sorts of evidence on the condition of the machine, wouldn't they? Well, the sheriff decided it would be best to get that data right now, before the machine has been used again. It's a simple thing, and no doubt an unnecessary thing, but it could be vital."

"Yes, yes. I see. At least for my part, I'm quite confident that I followed all the recommendations for maintenance, and I keep very good records. You can check out any of my machines."

Chuck interrupted with an irrelevant, "Yah, they look pretty good. What's your favorite?"

"Oh," Hoffman smiled, "I like the Cats."

Under other circumstances, Orly might have been annoyed with Chuck's interruption. But in this case it was a perfect diversion. Hoffman didn't have to know that in addition to checking the condition of the machine's controls, they might also check for fingerprints. Besides, Orly was beginning to see a possible line of inquiry.

"I doubt if anything will ever come of this, but in the event any witnesses are needed, can you give me a list of everybody that was at the resort that night?"

"Of course. You see, it was only the employees of Hofstead Hail and Mr. and Mrs. Hofstead themselves. That would be, um, Mr. and Mrs. Swenson, or whatever her last name is, Mr. and Mrs. Sandberg, that Finnish guy and his wife, and the Kvammes."

"And no one else was staying at the resort?"

"No, nobody except me and Sharon, that is."

"What about other guests in the restaurant?"

"I don't think that will be useful to you. Everyone was gone by nine o'clock. At that time the Hofstead company was still dining."

"Nevertheless, I'd still like their names," insisted Peterson, unwilling to leave an uncollected fact for which he could be criticized.

"I can give you the name of one couple, Peter and Angie Wahlstrom. I didn't catch the name of the other couple. I mean, Friday night is not usually a big night. Nobody has to call for reservations. People just show up. I think the Wahlstroms knew the other couple, though, so you could ask them. The Wahlstroms live in one of those year-round vacation homes near Dent. But like I say, all of them were gone by nine o'clock."

"Well, I'm sure we won't bother them. But it doesn't hurt to have this information just in case. And, you know, we are not insensitive to your business concerns. We'll do anything we can to ensure that this has no adverse effect on the Otter Slide."

Hoffman smiled and said with palpable relief, "My wife will be glad to hear that!"

It was a simple matter to load the snowmobile onto the trailer, and within a few minutes and more assurances to Hoffman that they would take care of the machine, Orly and Chuck were on their way back to Fergus Falls.

"Chicken fried steak!"

"I beg your pardon?" asked the somewhat bewildered Orly Peterson.

"I'm gonna have me a nice chicken fried steak."

"It figures," thought Orly.

SIXTEEN

PALMER KNUTSON LEANED BACK in his swivel leather chair and put his feet up on his desk. The office looked official enough, he thought, with the American flag and the State of Minnesota flag surrounding his new black steel desk. Behind his chair, on the wall between two windows, were a large map of Minnesota and a detailed map of Otter Tail County. On a special extension of his desk was the pride and joy of the Otter Tail County Law Enforcement Center, a new Macintosh computer. Palmer hated it. As his private comment on the machine, he had added a Disney screen saver. With his ten o'clock cup of coffee in his hand, he stared at Mickey Mouse and Donald Duck bouncing across the screen. He turned occasionally to watch the snow drift down outside the window.

"Maybe next year," he thought, "with Trygve off to college, maybe Ellie and I could just sneak down to Mexico for a couple of weeks during January or February. It's been so long since just the two of us went off together. Why, it hasn't been since ... We've never done it! Married almost thirty-six years and never had a trip to ourselves, unless you count a three-day honeymoon to Winnipeg! How did we let that happen?"

The sheriff was letting his mind wander because he was unconsciously avoiding thinking about the problem that had been bothering him all morning. "How am I going to bring this up to Martha Hofstead?" Pluto bounded across the screen. "I know what it is," he thought. "It was seeing that Gary Swenson and his wife at the funeral yesterday. No kids. If they're not off skiing in Montana, they're lying on the beach in Hawaii. Makes me sick. We used to lie on the beach, Ellie and I, but we could never enjoy it because we never knew when a kid would start to drown. Besides, a lake beach isn't quite the same as the sands off Diamond Head. But that's something we should do. 'Course, I suppose I should go on a diet so I don't look so flabby in a swimming suit. Maybe I should work out over the noon hour." This resolve lasted for a few seconds and then his train of thought turned to what to have for lunch.

Palmer knew he should be doing something more constructive, but he didn't feel like concentrating on another item of business until he found out about the snowmobile from the Otter Slide. It had been bothering him ever since he saw the photograph of the site of Hofstead's death. He just couldn't shake the feeling that he was viewing the scene of a crime.

Karl Lindbergh, of Lindbergh Snowmobile and Marine, had agreed to examine the Otter Slide Polaris. He had sold the machine in the first place, and was an expert mechanic. If anyone could discover how a snowmobile could travel fifty feet over deep snow after its rider had fallen off, it was Karl Lindbergh. Knutson didn't think he could.

As the sheriff was considering whether or not it would hurt to eat just half of a Hershey bar with his coffee, Orly Peterson came in. Orly was dressed, as usual, in his uniform, affecting a sharp, pressed, and shiny appearance that made Palmer tired. From the eagerness in his step, Palmer could assume the gist of his report, but went through the routine. "Is Lindbergh done looking at that machine?"

"He sure is."

"Well?"

"He says no way in hell could that machine get that far away all by itself."

"No evidence that the throttle was stuck?"

"Nope."

"No evidence that it could have momentum enough to get down to the lake?"

"Nope. He says it would be impossible."

The sheriff pushed up his glasses and scratched his nose. "Okay. Well, that's a whole new ball game, isn't it? How much of this situation could Lindbergh guess?"

"Karl's no dummy! He knew it was the machine Hofstead had been riding on when he was killed. He said the whole deal was fishy. I knew that he knew that we suspected murder. I just asked him to keep still about it, and said that if we heard any rumors about it we would know where they came from. By the way, he put in a claim for his time."

"That was generous and public-spirited of him. Did you accept it?"

"Yah, under the circumstances, it was almost like buying his silence. Are we going to pay it?"

"I suppose. It's probably money well spent, in that the whole presumption of non-accidental death hinges on it at this point. Sit down, Orly, we've got a crime to solve. By the way, have you figured out how the murder was committed yet?"

Orly grinned. "Yah. It's really very obvious when you think about it. I've got two alternate explanations. First, the murderer has a helicopter. In the dead of night he times his approach over Long Lake, where to my knowledge no helicopter has ever been seen before, in order to intercept John Hofstead in a snowmobile totally imperceptible from any other snowmobile from a height of more than ten feet. Then he uses a long cable to hook onto the snowmobile, without Hofstead catching on, and steers him into the big loon. When Hofstead falls off, he uses the cable to tow the snowmobile onto the lake. Everything fits. But maybe I've got a better explanation…"

"Well," Palmer acknowledged. "Your first explanation certainly fits the facts. What's your second theory?"

"There are two people on the snowmobile. Hofstead is either already dead or is unconscious. The murderer takes him on the snowmobile, drives over to the loon, and carefully goes close enough so that it looks like Hofstead is knocked off. Maybe he even holds Hofstead up for one last crack on the head by the loon as he goes by just to make the fall look natural. He goes down to the lake, gets off on the clear ice, and walks away. There are no tracks in the snow other than the tracks left by the snowmobile and by Hofstead's falling body. Anyone who came upon the scene would assume it had been an accident. All things considered, I guess I prefer the second alternative."

Palmer was proud of his deputy. "Very good. It might have been possible, by the way, to have found a trace of footprints on the ice if anyone would have thought to look for them. But…," the sheriff gestured to the snowy window, "not any more. No, I'm not blaming you for not looking for tracks on the bare ice. Nobody would have. In any event, what do we deduce from this?"

"What do you mean?" Orly asked, warily.

"Who done it?"

"How should I know? Do you mean to tell me you know who did it?"

"Of course not, but what conclusions can be made as to who, in general, may have done it?"

"Oh, I see. Well, it would probably have to be someone who had some experience with snowmobiles. Not that it takes a long time to learn how to operate one, but still, one would have to at least know how to start and stop the machine."

"Granted. Go on."

"It would probably have to be someone of some strength. To be sure, Hofstead was not a large man, but you would need someone who could at least haul a body aboard a snowmobile. Actually, I suppose any adult person could just about do that, but it would probably rule out children or the decrepit elderly."

"Okay. Let's rule them out. What else?"

"I suppose we can start talking about motives and such. The victim would almost certainly have to know the murderer. The murderer would also need to have the opportunity, of course."

"Ah. Now you're getting it. How does the method at least point to a rather limited circle of suspects?"

"I see. Sure. If the murderer gets off the snowmobile, where does he go? He would almost certainly have got on the sled at the Otter Slide, so he would almost certainly walk back there across the ice. There is always the possibility that an outsider came to the resort in the middle of the night and lured Hofstead away and murdered him, but it seems logical to assume that the murderer is one of the people who spent the night at the resort."

"Excellent. And what else do we know about this murderer?"

"I was thinking about that last night," Orly responded, with a trace of determination in his voice, "and the more I thought about it, the more sure I was that Lindbergh would find nothing wrong with that sled this morning. I reasoned that if it were murder, it was probably not done under the loon. Would this make it premeditated? Not necessarily, it could still have been a spontaneous action. But if a blow to the head were spontaneous, and if the blow did not kill him, the trip to the loon, where an unconscious man would certainly freeze to death, was a vicious act by a potentially dangerous person. Agree?"

"Yes," Palmer nodded gravely, "I think I do."

"Therefore," and at this Orly rather squinted up at Palmer in an appeal for approval. "Therefore, I think we should let everyone assume as long as possible that this has been ruled an accidental death. Anybody who is capable of killing in this manner is capable of killing again. Furthermore, we may get more genuine results investigating this if we let people assume we are just looking into an accident. The murderer may become uneasy about what he would consider undue attention, but everyone else may talk more freely than if they think murder was involved."

"My thoughts exactly. How do you think we should proceed?"

Orly was stunned. The sheriff had never been so solicitous of his opinion. Perhaps he was actually starting to gain the sheriff's respect. He remembered uneasily how he had neatly wrapped up another murder case—means, motive, opportunity—and had proudly presented his findings to the sheriff. Knutson had professed himself to be impressed by the reasoning but had quickly proceeded to totally absolve Peterson's suspect and reveal the true murderer. That episode had left the deputy with a desperate wish to be right when he opened his mouth. This time, he said, "I suppose the first thing to do would be to hold an autopsy. That could no doubt tell us if he was killed outright or if he died of freezing. It could also tell us whether he was killed while wearing his helmet or if that was added later. If the latter occurred he was almost certainly killed at another location. Finally, of course, it could give us a firm ground for proceeding with our investigations."

"And then?"

"Well, obviously we have to inform the Bureau of Criminal Apprehension in a case like this. Those boys don't mind coming up from St. Paul in the summer, but I don't know how they'll like a winter assignment. I imagine one of the first things they will do is to re-examine the machine and test for fingerprints. There aren't apt to be many prints on it, since everybody would be wearing mittens, but you never know. That will mean getting prints from the corpse and from everybody else who might have touched the machine—if they find any prints, that is."

"And then?"

"We have to find out more about the victim. Who is his lawyer? What's in his will? We have to answer the ultimate question of who benefits from the victim's death. It looks like we have a general idea of the means, a fairly narrow list of people who might have had the opportunity, and so we need to find a motive."

"Yup, that's exactly it!" Palmer said as he slapped the table. "I tell you, Orly. You've got a future in this business. Unfortunately, it's first things first. I have been sitting here for the last hour wondering how I should approach Mrs. Hofstead. 'You know that husband of yours we had a funeral for yesterday? Well, me and the boys would like to cut him open and see how he bought the farm.' There is just no good way to do this."

Orly had been basking in the praise of the sheriff like a puppy who had just brought in the newspaper. Unfortunately, he ruined the moment by blurting out, "Are we going to have to dig him up?"

"What?"

"Hofstead. Didn't they bury him?"

"No, they don't do that in the middle of winter anymore. They hold the whole service and they sort of pretend they bury the body. The funeral home takes care of everything and they have a simple interment when the frost is out of the ground."

"No kidding. How do they store them? Burrow a hole in a snowdrift?"

"You know, I don't think I'm going to take you along when I have to go talk to Mrs. Hofstead."

"Good."

"No, on second thought, that's just what I'm going to do. I spoke to her briefly at the funeral and she thanked me for the way the department had handled things. Since you did everything, she was referring to you when she mentioned tact and understanding.

For reasons best known to herself, she formed a favorable impression of you. I think you should be there."

"She said that? What a nice lady! You know, I really want to get the man who killed her husband."

"What makes you assume it was a man?"

"Well, everything we've said, I mean, strong, able to drive a snowmobile, you know, it would seem to be a man, wouldn't it."

"Orly, Orly, Orly. You were doing so well. Think about it. Mrs. Hofstead is not much smaller than her husband. They had ridden together on snowmobiles for years. Right there you've got your means and opportunity. And in any marriage there are times when motive rears its ugly head."

Orly could not help an impertinent, "Speaking from experience?"

The sheriff did not take undue offense, and merely replied with a patronizing, "Ah, you unmarried young pup. You know so little. Just wait until you are playing bridge with another couple and your wife leads with the wrong suit. Just wait until your wife leaves the garage door open and you have to go out and close it and you slip on the ice. Just wait until she has thrown away your old sweatshirt just because it had a little hole in it. It's a wonder any of us survive."

"But you can't seriously think Mrs. Hofstead killed her husband!"

"No, I don't think she did. In fact I'm reasonably sure she didn't. But I've been wrong on such things before. You just can't assume. In fact, it's partly because I like Mrs. Hofstead that I want to find the person who killed her husband. He was a decent man who made our community a better place. Murder shouldn't happen in our county. It happens in less blessed places. This isn't Texas or Florida, it's Minnesota, for Pete's sake! Murder is just so tasteless!"

Orly found that he was increasingly able to see the less public side of Sheriff Knutson. Here was a man who deeply cared about society and worried about how crime and violence upset what he considered to be the natural order. Increasingly, he was able to see in the sheriff a concern that ran deeper than the day-to-day chores of keeping the peace. He was a reformer, an optimist who was depressed when the core of his well-behaved Minnesotans let him down and acted like other people. Otter Tail County was not paradise, but it was closer to Eden than anyplace else, and Knutson wanted to keep it that way. He found himself nodding and repeating, "tasteless!"

"So," Palmer said, and straightened up in his chair, "I'll call Mrs. Hofstead to see if we can talk to her. Then I'll call the BCA and see when they can come up. Meanwhile, make sure that snowmobile is secure and call Jimmy Clark and ask him to set up an autopsy. If Mrs. Hofstead can see us this afternoon, I'd like to talk to her as soon as possible, so get a car ready and check back with me in half an hour. Oh, and start a file—names, addresses, phone numbers, and so forth—on everybody who was at the resort the night of the murder."

SEVENTEEN

"COME IN, SHERIFF. COME in, Mr. Peterson. Let me take your coats."

Knutson and his deputy handed their parkas to Martha Hofstead and appreciated the warmth of the house. It was an attractive house, not overly large, befitting a childless couple with an assured and comfortable income. Palmer admired Martha's taste, as evident in the foyer done in subtle shades of blue. Mrs. Hofstead ushered them into the living room and said, "Just sit down. I'll get us some coffee."

Knutson and Peterson looked at each other without speaking. Orly was glad that in situations like this he could count on the sheriff to do the talking. Martha Hofstead returned almost immediately with a thermal HotPot of coffee and a tray of cookies. "Oh," protested the sheriff, "you shouldn't have gone to such trouble."

"It wasn't any trouble. Really. People have been very kind. I have received dozens of cookies in the last few days." She seemed to choke up and whispered, "So kind. Really."

"We're very grateful that you took the time to see us," Palmer began tentatively. "I'm sure you're very busy."

Martha Hofstead sighed and said, "You would think so, wouldn't you. And maybe I should be. All these wonderful people sending condolences. Everybody saying, 'If there is anything I can do to help …' Well, what am I supposed to say? Yes, will you please bring John back to me? Everybody assumes that there will be all sorts of people over, but no one wants to come. Other people have children to help them. I have nobody. In the days before the funeral everyone called and Pastor Knutson—he's your brother, isn't he?—was here. But since I got back from the funeral yesterday, only one person has called, and that was Borghild Kvamme from the office. You know, it makes one take stock of one's life. John was all I had. I'm not into self-pity, and I'm not asking for any from you. But I am just so bewildered. What will I do now?"

"Martha, John will be missed by the whole community, and we all share your loss. I know it sounds empty to make these kinds of assurances, but you are a healthy and talented woman who can do just about whatever you set your mind on. I'm sure that your husband, who believed in insurance, left you well provided for. I know it won't be easy, but you have the capacity and the opportunity to enjoy the rest of your life." Palmer thought he sounded like an idiot.

Orly thought, "I wish I could say things like that."

Martha sniffed, and Palmer continued. "But we are here about something else, a very serious matter. This may come as a shock to you, but we think that your husband's death may not have been an accident."

Mrs. Hofstead looked up quickly. "What do you mean?"

126

Palmer looked embarrassed and said, "I mean, are you aware of anyone who may have benefited from your husband's death?"

"You mean ...?"

"Yes. We have reason to suspect that your husband was murdered."

Martha gasped and put a Kleenex to her eyes. Orly, who had become more cynical and more suspicious since his talk with the sheriff, observed her and decided her shock was real.

"What makes you say this?" she asked weakly.

"We have pretty much determined that it would have been impossible for your husband to have accidentally run into the loon and for his sled to have kept on going all the way back down to the lake. We think someone else was there, and that the someone else murdered him and made it look like an accident."

"But why? Who could ever want to kill John? He didn't have an enemy in the world. He was the consummate do-gooder. His basic goodness almost shamed me sometimes because I just felt, well, that I could never be that good."

Palmer reached forward and filled his coffee cup. Martha automatically smiled and offered the cookie platter around. "Here, have another."

"Please believe me that what I am about to ask is necessary," he continued. "It is vital that we find out how and where John died. It is probable that he was killed elsewhere and taken to the loon afterward. Mrs. Hofstead, I intend to ask for an autopsy on your husband's body."

Mrs. Hofstead sat in silence. No tears fell. Orly became conscious of a new emotion present in the room. There was still the overwhelming sorrow, but now it was joined by something else.

Was it fear, he wondered? Or was it something else, a determined anger? In any event, when she spoke, it was with complete control. "And you need my permission for that?"

"Technically, no. We can get a court order and proceed without your permission, which, in this case, I'm afraid we would have to do. But I don't want this out in the open. I don't want whoever killed your husband to think that we are unsatisfied that it was anything other than an unfortunate accident. Whoever the murderer may be, he is a potentially dangerous person. I don't think it likely that anyone is in any danger, but anyone who could do it once has the potential to do it again. And since we have no idea of a motive, I have no way of knowing if this is the end of it."

It took Martha several seconds to realize the significance of his words. With a start, she looked up and gasped, "You mean, I might be in danger?"

Palmer tried to summon up a protective tone for his voice and said: "Well no … no, I doubt it. I doubt if anyone is. But I can't be sure. So be safe. Keep your door locked and just be careful. Now, do we have your consent to an autopsy?"

Mrs. Hofstead winced and silently nodded.

"Thank you. I'll keep you posted on what we find out. I realize that we have already taken up much of your time." Knutson realized as he said this that he was being insensitive to Mrs. Hofstead's earlier protestations that she had too much time on her hands. Still, he pressed on. "But if we could just ask you a few more questions."

Martha did not let it pass. "Time? Time? That's all I have left is time. Fire away, Sheriff."

"Er, thank you. Um, who is your attorney?"

"Old Thomas Knappen, of Knappen, O'Brien, and Keefe."

"And he would have the details of the will?"

"Yes, although it is straightforward enough. John had some insurance policies that benefited various colleges and foundations, but all assets come to me. My will is essentially the same as his, to benefit John, of course. We had them drawn up at the same time."

"So—and I don't mean to suggest anything—no one benefited financially by your husband's death, other than you?"

"Yes, that's correct."

Knutson had been ready to leave off questioning Mrs. Hofstead at the first sign of grief and agitation. But there was something in the determination evident in the muscles of her face that encouraged him to go on. Orly was unobtrusively taking notes and the sheriff continued, "What is the condition of your company, Hofstead Hail?"

"It's never been better. We have had record earnings."

"But this company meeting at the Otter Slide. That was a new thing, wasn't it?"

Martha tilted her head as she looked up in surprise. "You mean you haven't heard what it was all about?"

Orly started to squeeze his pen. It would seem they were about to learn something important. The sheriff calmly encouraged a reply, "Suppose you tell us."

Martha paused for a few seconds, then took a deep breath and said, "A few days ago, John surprised everybody by deciding, all by himself, to retire. He was so delighted with his decision he could hardly wait to tell me. He was going to remain as a sort of chief executive officer of the company and let someone else run it for him. The last two weeks of his life were two of the happiest in my existence. We made plans for next year. We were going to spend our summers here, but we would be spending our winters in Florida. He brought home travel literature and we began to plan for all the things we would do in our retirement. We even talked about going there in March, to check out things for next winter and to take in a couple of Twins preseason games. According to the weatherman, these have been the two coldest weeks in years, and yet, planning for Florida with John, I've hardly noticed them. And now, well, now it seems colder than I can ever remember."

After a heavy silence, it was Peterson who asked, "Who was going to take over Hofstead Hail?"

It was a good strategic move in the interview process that allowed the powerful empathy that existed between Knutson and Mrs. Hofstead to be temporarily put aside so that she could answer a question from a different quarter. "Well," she said, with almost a trace of a smile, "that was the question. That was the whole purpose of our business retreat."

"How do you mean?"

"It was originally John's idea to meet with his whole company and to interview them all to see who would be the best president of Hofstead Hail. I think virtually all of the employees saw themselves as his successor. The whole thing was turning into a glorified beauty contest. I think John saw this as a fair way to start over and objectively survey the field and make the choice that was best for the company on the basis of what he had observed over the weekend. But he eventually abandoned that notion. In the end, he had made his decision and was going to use the time for an opportunity to allow the members of the company to get comfortable with the new president. He intended to announce his decision at breakfast on Saturday morning."

"Did you know his choice?" Palmer quietly asked.

Martha smiled at the irony. "Yes, in fact, that was almost the last thing he ever said to me. I think he may have made his mind up several days before, I don't know, but he enjoyed his little secret. He had asked my advice about each member of the firm and I told him what I thought. He just nodded noncommittally when I suggested a positive attribute of someone and gallantly defended them when I was critical. Anyway, by the time we finished supper on Friday night, John could see how the rest of the company was reacting to his weekend plans and he decided it was unfair to keep things going as they were. As he was getting ready to go out snow-mobiling he told me that he was going to get everyone together over breakfast and end all the speculation."

Orly looked up at Knutson, who subtly nodded. "And who," the deputy asked, "had he chosen run the company?"

Martha smiled. "He picked my choice. He appreciated my view and said that the more he thought about it, the more right I was. I loved him for it."

"Um, and who was that?"

"Borghild, of course. And she's still going to run the company."

Knutson could not hide his surprise. He had no real knowledge of the company, but had only considered Borghild, if he had considered her at all, to be merely an elderly secretary. "Borghild?" he asked.

If one can be said to be able to "stamp" an index finger, this is what Martha did on the coffee table. "Borghild! She is the only person who has seen the totality of the company. She is the only person that everyone else in the company could work for on an even level. Besides, Borghild has talent. If she would have had the opportunities that young women have today she would have been a lawyer or an MBA working for a large firm. I pointed out to John just how valuable she had been over the entire course of the agency. As John said, almost his final words to me, in fact, 'It's time we recognized what Borghild has done for us and what she can do in the future.'"

The implication hung in the air as Palmer asked, "Did he tell anybody else?"

Martha considered the question for some time before answering. "I doubt it. He told me to be sure not to tell anyone until he had made the announcement, so I doubt that he would have spilled the beans himself."

Palmer nodded and asked, "Did he tell Borghild?"

"Apparently he had planned to do so just before he announced it to the others. I told her yesterday that I wanted her to run the company. She was polite and grateful and said that she could probably run it for a while until I made up my mind who I wanted as a permanent president. I had to convince her that it was not just my choice, and not just a favor to me, but that she was John's choice for a permanent president." There followed a silence broken by a slight whimper. "…We had a good cry over it."

Knutson nodded again and asked, "Have you told any other members of the firm of your decision?"

"No. The agency has been closed, of course. I told Borghild to just carry on with the routine and to make whatever plans she needed to make. We will get everybody together later this week."

"I hate to make too much of this," Palmer said, "but just to be clear, at the time of your husband's death, each employee of the company thought that he or she might be the new president? No one had an inkling of who it might be?"

"As far as I know, that is correct."

As Orly wrote this last response in his book, he looked as though he had heard something of terrible significance. The sheriff stood up. "Thank you, Mrs. Hofstead. You have been most helpful. Remember that at this point your husband's death may have been an accident, and we are very reluctant to pursue this any further until we know more. Meanwhile, please don't say anything about this to anyone. If, indeed, this was all a terrible accident, well, then, we don't want to cause anyone anxiety. We will keep you informed as to our findings. Oh, and, er, thank you for the coffee and cookies."

The deputy put away his notebook and took Mrs. Hofstead's hands in his. "And allow me to say once again how sorry we are. If there is anything I can do, please do not hesitate to call."

The new widow mumbled her thanks and showed them out the door. The snow had let up, but the wind had risen, and Knutson and Peterson walked rapidly to the car. As they pulled away into the street, Peterson said, "Well, we got motive!"

Knutson responded with a hint of sarcasm. "You mean," he said, "someone wanted to be president of a small insurance firm enough that they would kill for it?"

Orly, now playing the realist, replied, "People have killed for less."

EIGHTEEN

AT TEN O'CLOCK ON the following day, two agents from the Minnesota Bureau of Criminal Apprehension appeared in the office of the sheriff of Otter Tail county. There had been a time when law enforcement agencies in "outstate" Minnesota resented the interference of the BCA, but that was mostly past. One of the main reasons for this was the activities of sheriffs like Palmer Knutson. Rather than resenting the expertise of the Bureau, Palmer welcomed it. As he said to Orly, "Look, those guys know what they're doing and they have equipment we could only dream about. Why should we inflate our county budget on things like that as long as they not only have that stuff, but they know what to do with it?" As an explanation, it may have been ineloquent, but it was to the point. Furthermore, over the years Palmer Knutson had gained a reputation in St. Paul as "the one county sheriff who knows what it's all about." The meeting between the sheriff and the BCA on this cold January morning was, therefore, warm. After exchanged pleasantries, during which the coffee was poured and Palmer assured them that Ellie was fine and the kids were doing great, they got down to business.

The agents were about the same age and size, so that, although facially they bore no resemblance to each other, there was an air of interchangeability about them. They exchanged glances before the first one spoke. "So, mechanically, the snowmobile checks out? Can you trust this guy, Lindbergh?"

"Yah," Knutson assured him, "I think I can. Look it over yourselves, of course, but this guy knows as much about snowmobiles as anybody. If you could just go over the machine for prints, I mean, that's really all there is to do with that. I've arranged for an autopsy for later today. You will want to go over the clothes the victim was wearing, I suppose. Other than that, I can't see that there is too much for you guys to do."

They both nodded in unison before the second agent spoke. "What about the scene where the victim was found?"

"I don't think it's even worth a visit. My deputy did take pictures before anything was disturbed. Since then, however, we got down there and removed the body and the snowmobile was taken back to the resort and then, after a couple of days, we brought it in here. Since the night in question, it has snowed several inches. Besides, I don't suppose you will feel too disappointed if you have to spend all of your time working inside, will you?"

It was impossible for any BCA agent to be as laid back as Palmer Knutson. There still existed that "don't try to tell us our job, we are the experts" mentality. They exchanged glances again before the first officer explained, "I'm sure you're right, Sheriff. But as long as we're here I think we should visit the scene where the body was found. Have you examined the loon, for instance? Have you determined where, if anywhere at all, the victim's head came into contact with the loon?"

Palmer patiently responded, "No, ah, we haven't looked for that. I suppose we should have checked that out?"

In the language of officialdom, the BCA agent explained, "We don't necessarily interpret all the data, but we like to collect all the data. Interpretations come later."

Knutson was already tired of this conversation. "Right. Well, I'll have my deputy take you down to where we have the snowmobile and I'll have the victim's clothes brought to you. I'll ask one of my deputies who was along when the body was removed to stand by to take you to the scene. His name is Chuck Schultz. Meanwhile, don't be afraid to ask anybody around here for whatever you need."

The agents did a well-choreographed rise and the second one mechanically jerked the sheriff's hand. "Thanks, Palmer. That ought to do for now. If we find any good prints on that machine, you know, we may need help in getting some prints from the principles involved for comparison purposes."

"Yah, well, I've already arranged for the prints to be taken from the deceased. They'll be taken at the time of the autopsy, which should be starting in a few minutes. I'll have them sent along."

Orly was on his way in as the BCA agents left Palmer's office. "So, are the high-tech nerds going to solve this case for us?" he asked, as soon as he was certain that the BCA agents couldn't hear him.

"One can hope. At least it might give us something to go on. Nothing seems to impress the juries on TV as much as the old fingerprint on the windowsill or the footprint in the flower bed. What have you got from Hofstead's lawyer?"

Orly plopped down on the chair in front of Palmer's desk. The sheriff noticed that he was, as usual, wearing his gun. Knutson questioned this habit most of the time, but decided that in the present circumstances it might be a good idea after all. Knutson never wore a gun if he could help it. In fact, he hadn't fired a pistol in over three years, and then it had been only at the practice range. From the time he had been an MP in the army, through his career as deputy sheriff and sheriff, he had never pointed a gun at anybody. He meant to keep it this way. On Orly, though, who prided himself on his marksmanship with a pistol, the gun looked natural, the perfect accessory to his precise uniform. Orly leaned back in his chair and Knutson knew he had picked up something interesting. "As a matter of fact," Orly began, "I discovered a little item that could be interesting."

"Yes?" prodded the sheriff.

"You know how Mrs. Hofstead said all assets passed to her? Well that's true enough, but she also said that Hofstead had a few life insurance policies that benefited colleges and foundations, right? Well, that was also true. To be sure, there was a nice policy that benefited Martha. And, there was a large life insurance policy that named Concordia College as a beneficiary, and another that named the Fergus Falls State University Scholar's Fund. But that wasn't all."

"Yes?" prompted Knutson.

"There was another life insurance policy naming someone else as beneficiary."

"Yes?" repeated the sheriff, growing a little more impatient.

"There was a policy in the amount of five thousand dollars for one Laura Epperly of Des Moines, Iowa," related Orly, with his eyebrows raised.

"So who's that?"

"I don't know, but it makes you think, doesn't it?"

"It apparently makes you think, in any event. What about it?"

"Well, here's this guy who owns an insurance agency. Des Moines is kind of an insurance town, isn't it?"

"Yah. So?"

Orly's eyebrows raised. "So, maybe he goes to Des Moines on conventions and he has a special friend there."

"Maybe she's his niece or something."

Orly smiled with a smugness that reflected the fact that he had anticipated the sheriff's objection. "I considered that, so I called up Mrs. Hofstead. I asked her if she had ever heard of a person named Laura Epperly. She said she hadn't."

"I see," the sheriff said, frowning. "So now you think Martha Hofstead finds out that her husband is engaged in some sort of hanky-panky with another woman and decides to wait until a winter evening to waste him. That it?"

"Well, yah," Orly retorted. "You always ask, 'Who benefits?' Clearly, the wife benefits. She gets all the assets before her husband has a chance to do her out of them by taking up with another woman."

Knutson made a helpless gesture and asked, "Is that the impression that you got from talking to Martha Hofstead—that she could go out and kill her husband?"

"Now who's being the sentimentalist! And, for that matter, what about this Epperly woman? She could have knocked off Hofstead for the five grand!"

"Five thousand dollars is not the sort of princely sum for which one commits murder, is it?"

"Oh, I don't know. As I said before, murder has been done for less."

"All right then, you go and find out all about her. Call the cops in Des Moines. See if you can find out the relationship between her and Hofstead. And Orly, don't go bothering Mrs. Hofstead again without checking with me first. I admit that you have a certain amount of cruel logic on your side, but she's still the grieving widow. We need to be on the same page on this."

"Yah, sorry. But I did deal with her in a sympathetic way, I really did. So, I'll find out about that woman. What are you going to be doing?"

"Lunch."

In the summertime, when the population of Otter Tail county swells with hoards of vacationers who take up residency in the A-frames and bungalows that surround the clear lakes, Palmer Knutson rarely had time for a leisurely lunch hour. This situation changed in the winter. Over the last few winters, as Palmer began to adopt a more stop-to-smell-the-roses kind of existence, he had started to extend his lunch hours. Ellie, who had a part-time job in the municipal library, was able to adjust her schedule to match that of her husband. It had come to be a favorite time, a time when they were able to share a sandwich and conversation at Mabel Murphy's Restaurant, or maybe just have lunch at home. Both locations were romantic. Sometimes, in fact, they were so romantic that they skipped lunch altogether.

On this cold January day, however, Palmer's morning idling had been focused on the beef soup that he had had the night before. It was a wonderful mixture of beef and onions and potatoes and carrots, and it was the kind that got better every day as it was reheated. Ellie had it bubbling on the stove when he came in, and as he kissed her, he couldn't decide whether he was more attracted to the scent of his wife's perfume or her soup. Eagerly he sat down, hoping the experience of one of his favorite culinary repasts would wipe away a vague and gnawing depression. Ellie watched him butter and re-butter two slices of toast. She enjoyed watching him eat, watching the satisfied glow that covered his face as he turned all his attention to the enjoyment of the moment. Yet, as she waited for the effusion of satisfaction that usually enveloped him at such moments, she was aware that something was wrong. To be sure, her husband was enjoying his soup, but in total repudiation of his usual tradition, he was thinking of something else. She was curious. "What is it, dear?"

"Huh?"

"What's the matter?"

"I'm thinking maybe I should retire."

Whatever Ellie was thinking might be the matter, she was unprepared for that. Nevertheless, she took the announcement calmly. "Really, why's that?"

"Sometimes I don't like my job any more. I sort of wish I'd become a teacher after all. That's what I was thinking of once, you know. Maybe it's not too late."

"Well, let's think about it," answered Ellie in that too-rational tone of voice. "What would you like to teach?"

"I was going to be a history teacher one time."

"Okay, so you want to quit being sheriff and be a history teacher. The money is better as sheriff, you know."

"Money isn't everything."

"Of course not. So, to be a teacher you have to go back to college. What kind of teacher do you want to be? If you would want to be a teacher at the university you need to get a PhD. Now, to get that would be at least a four-year commitment. Four years of paying tuition, and meanwhile you have no income. Not a good prospect with Trygve going off to college himself next year. Besides, where would you go? What kind of university would accept an old sheriff into their graduate program? I'll tell you what kind, the kind of university you wouldn't want to go to. But even if you get in, then what? There are no jobs out there and even if there were, how would you like the prospect of turning into a nerdy little toad like your old favorite at FFSU, Harold Winston? How does that coincide with your self-image?

"Okay, so the doctorate is not for you. What about an MA? You could maybe even pick that up at good old Fergus Falls State. Then you would be qualified to teach at some community college, if you had teaching experience, which you don't. How many jobs do you suppose are out there? Do you know what most people who have their master's degree in history are doing now? They are selling insurance. So take two years out of your life, years with all outgo and no income, and then you can ask Mrs. Hofstead for a job. Palmer, are you listening?"

In spite of himself, Palmer had to smile. He did love his wife.

"So maybe higher education isn't the ticket. How about secondary education at the junior high or senior high level? Fine, but it has been thirty-five years since you were in college. You'd have to go back and get certified and you'd have to practice teach. That's at least a year of full-time college. And think about it. There has been a powerful lot of history going on in these last thirty-five years. You'd have to brush up on your coursework. But, of course, you can't just go out and earn a teaching certificate and get a job in a high school. No, you might be a great teacher, but you also have to be someone who can deflect switch blades, operate a metal detector, and do pregnancy counseling. You may be able to take your average student with the intellectual curiosity of a corpse, hold a mirror under his nose, find a faint pulse, and teach him who the president is, but nobody really cares. The first question you hear is, 'What can you coach?' And so you have to go back to college to pick up a coaching minor. Can you see yourself sitting in class with a bunch of nineteen-year-old boys learning the art of coaching basketball?"

Palmer was chuckling now, but Ellie was not done.

"Junior high? If you want to do that, the first thing you should do is have a rigorous exam—of your head! We're talking seventh and eighth graders here, we're not talking about true *homo sapiens*. And do you think you could teach them history? Ha! And I say again, ha! There's not time for that. You teach them rudimentary geography, civics, current events, man in the ecosystem, dating made safe. In other words, you teach Social Studies. Social Studies, Palmer. Social Studies! Uffda."

Palmer's good humor had been restored. "Okay, maybe I won't quit and become a teacher. Maybe I can be the sheriff for a couple more years."

But Ellie knew that the source of Palmer's discontent had not been removed. Her soft green eyes smiled in compassionate empathy, and she asked, "Really, though, what's bothering you?"

"Murder."

"So there's no doubt anymore?"

"The autopsy is being performed now, and that can probably make it certain, but I really have no doubt. You know, I was sheriff for a long time before I had my first murder case, and that was, well, I could understand how that happened. In that case, the victim had made a lot of enemies. Four or five years earlier there was that kid who was shot in a burglary attempt, when everybody just lost their head and nobody thought to call us until it was all over. Totally unpremeditated, in any event. But this! John Hofstead! A guy who gave back more to his community than he took from it. What kind of person can willfully and deliberately take the life of another? That's not supposed to happen here."

After a lengthy pause, the sheriff continued. "But you know what's worse? I've probably already met the murderer. He's one of us. He goes down and buys his Wheaties at our grocery store, he buys his mouse traps at our Target, he eats at our McDonald's. And how do I find out who it is? I have to lay bare the lives of everyone involved.

"Just this morning Orly found out that there was a life insurance policy among John Hofstead's effects that benefited a woman who lives in Des Moines. Immediately Orly gets his imagination all humming and calls up Martha Hofstead to see if she knows anything about it. Of course she doesn't, and Orly starts speculating about a filthy little liaison. I mean, here's John Hofstead, who lived his life as the perfect model of a Christian gentleman, and within a few hours of his funeral the sheriff's office is digging dirt.

"And that's just the beginning," Palmer continued, waving his spoon around. "If indeed he was murdered, then all circumstances surrounding his death indicate that it was done by someone who was staying at the Otter Slide Resort that night. That means that over the next few days I have to talk to these people and peel back their private lives to see if their very private actions include murder. More than likely the murderer acted alone, so that means the others' lives will be needlessly intruded upon."

The clock in the living room beat out the Westminster chimes and informed them that it was now one o'clock. Palmer waited until the last gong had faded. "I didn't become a sheriff to do that. I became a sheriff to help Farmer Johnson find out who rustled his cow. We find out who the kids were who broke into a beer truck so we can straighten 'em out before they do anything worse. We catch some burglars and maybe scare off many more, and we are there to intervene in cases of domestic violence. I mean, most of the time I go to bed satisfied that I really helped people. But murder investigations! I have to go out this afternoon and start grilling people, most of whom will be totally innocent and did nothing to bring this down on their heads. It's not going to be pleasant."

Ellie said, with tongue firmly in cheek, "Why don't you turn the case over to Orly?"

"I know you mean that only as a joke, but Orly could handle it. He's come a long way in the last year. He's acquired tact and a little imagination. As difficult as this may be to believe, considering what I used to say, I like the guy. In fact, he said something about this case that I thought was really perceptive. Unfortunately, I thought so at the time and now I can't, for the life of me, remember what it was. I just wish that he wasn't such a, well, such a Swede."

"Well, he can hardly help that, dear, now can he?"

"I suppose not. But sometimes I wish he would try to be—and only another Norwegian could really appreciate what I mean—a little less of a Swede."

NINETEEN

"You know, we could just as well have walked. We probably won't find a parking place much closer," said Orly Peterson, as he and the sheriff headed toward the old Kaddatz Hotel building. Knutson grunted and parked his Acura Integra immediately in front of the building.

"What was that again?"

"Never mind."

"You gotta learn to plan ahead, Orly. What if we want to go someplace from here? We would have to walk all the way back to the office just to get the car, and who wants to walk around in this wind?"

That was no small consideration. The wind caught Knutson's door and whipped it open wide into the street. A van, with a windshield almost totally frosted over, nearly tore it off the hinges. The cold air almost took the sheriff's breath away. "Besides," he gasped, "remember my rule of longevity. 'Never walk if you can ride, never stand if you can sit.'"

"And never sit when if you can lie down," completed the deputy. "Are you going to mention to anyone that we are now investigating a murder?"

"Nah, not directly at least. Let them figure it out. It's generally a good rule of thumb in an investigation not to tell people any more than they need to know."

When Knutson had returned to the office that afternoon, the autopsy had been completed. Stripped of its technical terms, a process in which Jimmy Clark excelled, the report stated that John Hofstead had been wounded by a blow to the back of the head by an unknown instrument, but that he had, in fact, frozen to death. As the medical examiner had pointed out, this was totally inconsistent with a head injury that would have been sustained by an accidental collision with the loon. In such a case, it would have been virtually impossible for the victim to be injured in such a way unless he had been riding at high speed while looking backward. Once that had been rather easily determined, the medical examiner decided that the wound was consistent with a blow from a narrow, heavy object, such as a tire iron or a wrench. The time of death was, at this late date, impossible to determine, but the medical examiner estimated that the blow would have been sufficient to render the victim unconscious. It was his opinion that the victim would not have regained consciousness before he was brought out to the loon. Of course, there was no way of knowing that for sure.

The BCA agents had also stopped in shortly before Knutson and Peterson left the office. They were on their way to view the scene where the body had been found and promised a full written report on the next day. Meanwhile, there was little to report concerning evidence from the snowmobile. They had found three sets of fingerprints on the machine, one of which matched those of the victim. They had also examined the helmet and a large, flat plastic zipper pull from the victim's snowmobile suit. The victim's fingerprints were found on both items, and in the case of the helmet, the other two sets of prints were also found. On the plastic zipper pull, a novelty item that contained a small outdoor thermometer, fragments of a fingerprint, identical to one found on both the snowmobile and the helmet, partially covered those of the victim. It would seem that someone other than the victim had been the last one to zip up the suit.

The sheriff could think of no good reason for delaying his inquiries, so in spite of the lateness of the afternoon and the nasty wind, he collected his deputy and decided to begin his interviews with the surviving personnel of Hofstead Hail. The entry into what had been one of the grandest hotel lobbies in the state was made with a minimum of heat loss, but in its state of partial preservation the building was still cold. They wasted little time in climbing the stairs to the third floor.

Unlike the chilly hallway, the offices of Hofstead Hail enveloped them in the warm, moist coziness of steam heat. Behind her desk, Borghild Kvamme sat, stoically going through the personal files of her erstwhile boss. She looked up as she saw them enter, and indicated no surprise that the sheriff should visit her. After all, sheriffs need insurance, too, and the agency did quite a lot of business with the county. "Good afternoon, Sheriff. What can I do for you today?"

Knutson removed his black furry Russian hat and said, "Hello, Mrs. Kvamme. Have you met Orly Peterson, one of my deputies?"

"Yes, we met briefly last Saturday morning out at the resort. How are you, Mr. Peterson?"

Orly self-consciously whipped off his woolen Norwegian ski cap, a hand-knitted Christmas present from his girlfriend Allysha, and mutely nodded his greetings.

Knutson continued, "We're, uh, just looking into a few things concerning Mr. Hofstead's death—terrible thing, wasn't it?—and we want to talk to everybody who was out at the resort that night. I understand the whole company was there?"

Borghild nodded and gestured to a pair of chairs. "Please, sit down. Would you like a cup of coffee? Of course you would, coming in on a day like this." Knowing better than to ask if anyone in Fergus Falls, Minnesota, would want cream or sugar, she poured coffee into two Hofstead Hail mugs. Extending the coffee cups to two rather eager hands, she responded, "Yah, we were all there. We even had all of the wives along, and I brought Harry along."

"Was this the first time you had ever done anything like this as a company?" Knutson asked.

"Of course, but then, this was something special, wasn't it? I mean, John had told everyone that he was going to retire and that he had decided to hire a new president among the current personnel. Everybody saw it as a chance to convince the boss that he was the man for the job."

"What about you, Mrs. Kvamme? Did you go out there with the idea of 'campaigning for the presidency' as it were?"

"Ha! That was the last thing on my mind. Although, I was telling Harry that John could do worse than to pick me. But really, you know, I sort of felt that I was asked along as a courtesy, you know, the old secretary can't be left out. But I told Harry, I told him, 'What the heck? How many chances do we get to go off on a retreat with all the meals paid?' We aren't exactly busy in January. Who is? But I could sure tell that Clarence and Pek and Young Gary were campaigning! And their wives! They were even worse."

"When did you first get an inkling that Mr. Hofstead meant to appoint you as president?"

"Inkling? I never had the slightest inkling. I went to visit Martha to see how she was doing and she told me. In fact, I wasn't so sure I believed her then. I thought that maybe she didn't want anybody else to take over and so she just made up the idea that John had picked me. I agreed to do it at the time because I didn't want to upset her more, but I figured that after the funeral, when things had time to settle down, she would change her mind and decide to leave it to Clarence or somebody. Well, anyway, that's how I felt until today. I thought I'd better go through all these papers to see what we should keep and what we should clean out, and I came across John's version of a real flow chart. If you knew John, you would know that things like that were extremely out of character, but I think he had got all wrapped up in this idea of being a CEO. So anyway, I came across this chart that he had drawn up with me as the president and those three guys all working under me. I thought, 'Hey, if John had that kind of confidence in me, why not?' You have just witnessed one of the most rapid rises in business history—from secretary to president in one fell swoop!"

"I guess congratulations are in order," Knutson smiled. "Tell me, do any of the others know that you are to be the new president?"

"Not unless Martha has told them, and she said she wouldn't until our meeting on Friday. I've hardly seen anybody myself, what with the funeral and the fact that business is slow in January anyway."

"Would you mind running through the events of that weekend with us?"

"Of course not, but why, what's the matter?"

Knutson assured her that they were just making routine inquiries, but the overly dismissive "tut-tut-tutting" of Orly Peterson made the new insurance executive suspicious. Her eyes narrowed and she nodded in comprehension. "Very well, I'll tell you what I can remember."

"How long ago was this retreat planned?" the sheriff asked.

"Only about two weeks in advance. John just decided one day to retire. He didn't talk it over with Martha or anything. Apparently the moment he decided to retire he called up the Otter Slide and booked the weekend. As soon as he got off the phone to them, he called us in and told us his plans."

"Were you surprised?"

Borghild considered the question briefly before responding. "We all were. Not only because John had decided to retire, but because of the speed in which he acted. John just didn't do things that way. He was a very deliberate person. It wasn't that he was so conservative— in many ways he was fairly liberal in his thinking—but he never did anything rash."

"Was this weekend greeted with enthusiasm?" the sheriff asked. "Did you and the other people want to go?"

"Enthusiasm? Well, maybe not by everyone. In fact, the only one who seemed really enthusiastic about it was Gary Swenson. But then, he's enthusiastic about everything. Still, nobody was against it either. None of us had ever done anything like that before. I didn't think I could talk Harry into going along with me, but he surprised me by being quite willing to go."

Knutson gave kind of a boyish shrug and said, "I suppose you think I'm really nosy about that weekend, but nobody can figure just what John was doing out there by the loon. I think it would ease Martha's mind a little bit if we could find out, don't you? And I'm just wondering if anything happened that night that could have caused him to go off like that. Now, you say everybody but you was sort of figuring up their odds of being picked to be the new president. Who did you think Hofstead would pick?"

Borghild held out both of her hands with the palms turned up. "I thought it would be either Clarence or Gary; I think everybody did. Pek is a nice guy, and everybody likes him, but nobody likes him really well. Know what I mean? It's kind of hard to explain. He does good business for the company and he could probably be successful as a president. In fact I'm sure he could. But no one would ever really think of him. Clarence, on the other hand, seemed in a position to inherit the job. He certainly thought he would be named. You could just see the dislike he had for Gary, and he slyly kept referring to Pek's boozing. Listen, Pek might like a nip now and then, but he has never let it interfere with his work and I'm going to make sure he stays with us. Gary, too, annoying as he can be sometimes. Clarence never bothered to think of me as presidential timber. Gary either, for that matter. Gary probably fed all the data into his computer and it came out 'Gary.' I might add that I think it was some pretty carefully selected data. I think if Clarence were going to be the president, I'd have stayed on a couple of years to help him out, but if Gary were going to run the company, I'd have retired. I'm sure that would have pleased Gary, too. Now, ironically, the one I'm most worried about is Clarence. Can he accept a woman as his boss?"

Knutson deftly avoided the question and asked one of his own. "Could you feel any tension as this weekend approached?"

"Oh, yah. I think so. Everybody seemed to feel a little funny on Friday night. We were the last to get there, and the rest had all gone to their rooms by the time we came. I think a few of them managed to get to the bar before supper, but we barely had time to check out our room and get ready to eat, so we really didn't talk to anyone privately. We ate a little after six thirty, I guess, and that was nice enough. I did notice one thing, though. I had gotten the impression that John was really looking forward to the weekend, sort of a grand finale to his career, so to speak. But at the table, when others were loosening up and having a good time, John, who is usually the life of the party, sat rather quietly. He looked preoccupied throughout the whole meal."

"Was he that way the last time you saw him?"

"You know, I think he was. After the dinner he got up and said a few words and then seemed to put on this hearty 'let's go have some fun' attitude. But it didn't seem real."

"And you didn't go out for a snowmobile ride?"

"Don't be silly. Riding around on a cold lake in the middle of the night? My generation does everything we can to avoid that!"

"John Hofstead was your generation."

"Ha!" Borghild retorted. "Sometimes I wondered! Still, I suppose that was one of the things I really liked about the man."

"Haven't you ever been on a snowmobile?"

"Of course I have. Harry, you know, was quite an enthusiast for a while about fifteen years ago. Then he just got tired of it. It's been years now since either of us has driven one. In our time, though, we enjoyed it. We used to go around Maplewood State Park all the time."

"So you and Harry didn't go out, and the only others who didn't go were Mrs. Hofstead and Iris Pekanen, is that right?"

"I suppose so, although Harry and I just went back to our room and went to bed. I didn't see either Iris or Martha."

"Could you hear the snowmobiles coming and going?"

"Lord! Who couldn't? It didn't bother Harry. He was soon snoring away. I laid awake for quite a while, and I heard at least one of them come back. I fell asleep shortly after that, but I woke up about one o'clock when I heard another machine. I remember that because I looked at the clock radio and thought how silly it was to be out at that time. And I remember thinking, 'that thing seems to be going back out on the lake again.' Do you suppose that was John? Or, I mean, that John was on that sled?"

"Yah, from what we can guess, it probably was. What did you think on Saturday morning when he was nowhere to be found?"

"To tell you the truth, I wasn't all that worried. Martha claimed his half of the bed hadn't been slept in and all that, but I just thought that John had gotten up early, tidied up his half, and had gone out snowmobiling again. He had an amazing amount of energy for a man his age. I can't tell you how much I am going to miss his happy pink face around here. But anyhow, Gary Swenson wasn't around either and he had seemed to be the most enthusiastic snowmobiler the night before, so I thought that he was off trying to butter up the boss. It was only after he came in with his wife that I started to get uneasy."

"Yah, it sounds like it was a terrible morning. Well, you've given us a real good picture of what happened that night. I think we'll just ask around among the others to see if they can add anything. Is Harry at the lumberyard this afternoon?"

"I suppose so. They don't close for another hour or so. Do you want me to call and find out?"

"Nah, that's okay," Palmer reassured her. "We were going out that way anyhow. We might stop by for a second if we get a chance. If we don't, just give him our best and if he thinks of anything have him give us a call. Thanks for your help. We'll just look into this a couple of days and then let you get your lives back to normal. And Borghild, good luck in the new job."

"Thanks, Palmer," she smiled bashfully. "I might need it."

As they gathered their coats and fumbled with their hats, Orly, who had been silent the entire time, remembered his manners and thanked Borghild for the coffee. When they came outside, they were unprepared for the cold wind, which sucked their breath away. Orly managed to gasp, "So, are we really going to see Harry?"

Knutson jumped into the car, started the engine, and rolled the window down an inch to keep the frost from forming on the inside of the windshield. "Yah, we might as well. I don't think we're going to learn much, though."

There was not a single customer in the Fergus Falls Building Center. As they entered, Harry Kvamme was absently rearranging dowels in a rack at the back of the room. Knutson, although younger than Harry, understood the tact and pace required for a real Norwegian-American conversation. They dissected the weather, and last year's weather, and the weather in the winter of 1966. Palmer talked about the cold and Orly feigned a genuine interest and added how he once got frostbite himself when he went skiing when he shouldn't have. That all brought about snowmobiling and the cold night at the Otter Slide Resort. Palmer did not bother to explain why they were looking into those events, and it seemed to Harry that it was just part of the conversation. Harry was unable to give any opinion as to who he thought was going to be the president of Hofstead Hail, "'Cept I knew it vasn't going tew be Borghild! Boy, I sure vas wrong about dat. I yust didn't tink Hofstead vould let a voman do da yob, but yew know she vas da best von all along."

"We were talking to Borghild earlier today, about how the snowmobiles were coming and going all night," Knutson said. Then, to Orly's surprise, he added, "Yah, but I think Borghild said you got up and went outside that night?"

"She said dat? I tot she vas asleep da whole time. I voke up, musta been after von o'clock, and I could hear her sleeping avay. I laid dere for a while and den I tot, 'I tink I'll do a little reading, see if I get sleepy again.' So I got dressed and vent down tew da lobby and read a vhile."

"Did you see anybody else?"

"No, I don't tink so."

"Did you hear anybody?"

"Not den, but after a vhile I got sleepy, yew know, and I vent back to da room. Yust as I vent back tew bed I tot I heard someting in von of dose sheds. I tot, 'Yimminy dat's late tew be fooling around on a snowmobile. Dose people should go tew bed.'"

Palmer glanced up at Orly and then asked, "Do you have any idea who it was?"

"Nope."

"Well, it's been nice talking with you, Harry. We'll see you around."

"Yah, Harry," Orly added, "Keep varm. I mean, warm!"

"Yew bet," Harry assured him.

As they left the building center, Orly gulped into the wind, "You fibbed to the old codger! You said Borghild told you he got up in the night. You lecture me about integrity and then you lie like a rug!"

Palmer started to open the driver's side door and spoke to his deputy over the roof of the car. "No, I said 'I thought' Borghild said that. I will freely admit that sometimes I think wrong."

"Ah," muttered Orly, with reluctant admiration.

TWENTY

As they drove out of the Building Center parking lot, Orly said, "That old Harry, he's an original, isn't he? I get a kick out of his accent. It sounds like he stepped off the boat from Norway just last week."

"Yah, but he's a nice old guy."

"Of course he's a nice old guy, I didn't say he wasn't. But you know what's funny? When you start talking to him for a while, you start talking in that brogue yourself. It's like one of those Norwegian routines they do on the radio. Like, you know, when Ole and Sven went fishing that time."

"Oh, no, here it comes," groaned Palmer, inwardly.

"So they went to this resort on Big Cormorant Lake to do a little fishing, and they rent a boat and for hours they don't even get a nibble. They find this little cove where they start pulling in fish after fish. Well, they soon get way over their legal limit and figure they'd better quit and so Ole, he says, 'We got to remember dis place.' And Sven, he says, 'Yah, but how are yew going to remember it den?' And Ole says, 'Ve'll yust mark an X on da side of da boat.' So Sven stares at him for a long time and says, 'Dat's da dumbest ting yew've ever said, Ole. Dat vould never verk. How do yew know ve'll get da same boat?' You two guys sound just like that!"

"So what?" replied the sheriff, with a trace of testiness.

"Nothing," said Orly, defensively. "I just get a kick out of it, that's all. But, you know, by admitting that he left the room to go someplace else, supposedly to read so he didn't wake Borghild, he destroyed any alibi he might have had for the most likely time of the murder."

"Oh, come on, not Harry!"

"You're the one who always says to suspect everybody, not me. Borghild probably makes more money at her job than Harry makes at his. He thinks Hofstead is going to name somebody else as president and his wife will lose her job or will quit. There goes his meal ticket. There's your motive, and we've just found out his opportunity. Besides, you can tell how Borghild felt about John. Maybe Harry thought it was something else and he becomes a jealous husband." Orly was laughing at these last words, but Palmer actually nodded in agreement.

"Silly as it sounds, you're right. We have to leave open that possibility. But at the same time, if Harry takes away his alibi by saying he left the room, he also takes away Borghild's alibi. Right? If he is away for a while, who's to say that Borghild didn't get dressed, sneak out, and kill her boss? Maybe she had been embezzling funds for several years and with Hofstead retiring, an audit would reveal her guilt. Or maybe you're right, maybe she had been having an affair with Hofstead and now he was trying to end it. Keep in mind, though, we did learn one interesting fact this afternoon.

Both Borghild and Harry have had experience with snowmobiles. Both had means and opportunity, and we have just manufactured motives for each."

Orly was suddenly serious. "Yah, it does fit, doesn't it? You don't suppose that they really could have …"

Palmer laughed, "Of course not. But as an example of imaginative detecting, it's a honey of a theory."

"So, what are we going to do next?"

"It's ten after five on a cold day in January. It's dark, the wind is howling, and most places are closing. What do you suggest?"

"Go home?" Orly said, hopefully.

"You bet! Let's just stop by the office and see if there is any news and then leave it for another day."

Back at the Law Enforcement Center, Knutson discovered the two BCA agents waiting in his office. "I thought you guys were going to go up to Vergas and take a look around and then go back to St. Paul? Did you find out anything?"

"Yeah, we found out it is a dumb idea to go driving around in the country in the middle of a blizzard. We got as far as Pelican Rapids and then we decided to turn around. The way the wind is blowing the snow around, we decided that there wouldn't be much to see there anyway, and your on-the-scene men seem to have done a good job. The more we thought about it, the more we figured that we didn't want to spend the night in Vergas. As it was, we barely made it back to Fergus Falls. We're going to have to spend the night here again."

Palmer kindly said, "You're welcome to spend the night at our house."

The other agent, hitherto silent, now broke in, "No, no, that's all right. We can still get rooms for another night at the Comfort Inn.

But thank you though. That's very kind." Palmer was almost, but not quite, able to conceal his look of relief. "Tell you what, though, there is one thing you can do for us." Palmer once again looked worried. "You can get us an example of the fingerprints of that guy at the resort. As we told you, we came up with three different sets of prints. Now, we know one set belongs to the victim. We assume that another set will belong to that guy at the resort who equipped all the guests and who brought the sled back on Saturday. That will leave one set unaccounted for.

"If you could go out to that resort and get a set of his finger-prints, we could take them back with us to the lab and do some comparisons. We could isolate and concentrate on that one set of prints unaccounted for. Think you could get them for us by, say, noon tomorrow?"

"Yah, I can do that," Knutson agreed amiably, "if the wind goes down and the snowplows get out."

"Right, then. See you tomorrow."

"They seem like nice guys," Orly said as the two men left the office. "By the way, do you want me to come with you out to the Otter Slide?"

"Of course. After all, I've never been there before. You can introduce me. But we'll do that tomorrow. Let's call it a day!"

Nothing short of a murder would have dragged Palmer Knutson out of his cozy home on a night like that. Fortunately, Otter Tail County had already had its share of murders for the next twenty years, or so the sheriff assumed. Palmer's rest was undisturbed.

The next morning was bitter cold. A pair of sundogs guarded a sun that hung uselessly in the southern sky, providing hazy illumination and no heat. The snowplows had been at work since early in the morning and Palmer was able to get out of his driveway after Trygve had done a minimum of shoveling. The thought occurred to Knutson that next year his son would be in college and would be unavailable to shovel the driveway. Perhaps it was time to buy a snowblower. He had kept the engine heater plugged in all night, of course, and the Acura started without hesitation. It was still cold inside the car, however, and soon frost was sticking to the black rabbit fur of Knutson's cap. The tires, square in the cold, made a thumping noise as he pulled away from the house.

Orly was waiting for him in his office. Although he had removed his knit hat and parka, he still had his boots on. "You look ready to go," Knutson said as he removed his own coat. "But what say we have another cup of coffee first."

Orly took the hint and went out to the main office and returned with two cups, gave one to the sheriff, and sat down and made himself comfortable. "By the way, how are you going to get those prints? Are you just going to come out and ask for them?"

"No, I don't think that will be necessary. You know what really takes on some nice prints? Glossy photographs. I figured I'd just take along those pictures you took around the loon and ask Hoffman some questions about how he thought the snowmobile got so far away, you know, general talk like that. Then I'd hand him the pictures—downside, so he'd have to use his fingers to turn them over, and we'd have some nice prints."

"Brilliant! Meanwhile, we just interview him like any other suspect?"

"Sure. And as soon as you're done slurping your coffee, we can get going."

The drive to the Otter Slide was uneventful. For the most part, the road was in good winter driving condition, and snowplows were needed only in those sheltered areas where drifts had formed. The sheriff had not called ahead to ask for an appointment, deciding that a surprise visit might prove more useful. It might prove to be a wasted trip if no one were around, but, Palmer reasoned, where would a resort owner go on a cold January morning? This was sound reasoning, for they noticed as they drove into the resort that theirs were the first tire tracks to disturb the pristine white snow.

When David Hoffman answered their knock, he appeared to be indeed surprised to see them. It seemed to Orly that he almost slammed the door in their face. He caught himself in time, however, and managed a weak, "Oh, ah, Deputy, uh, Peterson, isn't it?"

"That's right," Orly replied, pushing past him. "And this here's Sheriff Palmer Knutson. Mind if we ask you a few questions?"

It seemed to Knutson that Hoffman was incapable of making up his mind what to do next. He finally said, unnecessarily, "Uh, come in. I'll go get my wife."

Before he could be stopped, he had disappeared with a pitiful whine, "Sharon, Sharon, can you come here for a minute? The sheriff is here."

Knutson looked up at Peterson and shrugged. Orly responded with, "He's sort of a jumpy little guy. He was that way when Schultz and I were out here on Saturday. It's like he needs to get permission from his wife for everything he says. By the way, did you notice his slippers?"

"Yah. Those are just like the ones we bought Trygve for Christmas when he was in fourth grade, and he just loved them. I wonder if he still remembers. I'll have to ask him and tell him that the proprietor of the Otter Slide Resort wears bear-paw slippers."

Sharon Hoffman came in with a determined, businesslike and not altogether friendly manner, with her husband trailing behind her. Her brown corduroy jeans, white Irish sweater, and fleece-lined moccasins had a mannish quality about them, as if to emphasize who was in charge. She came straight to the point. "Yes? Can we help you?"

Palmer decided that if he wasn't going to be asked to sit down, he would have to take the initiative himself. "If we could sit down and discuss a few things relating to the unfortunate death of Mr. Hofstead last weekend?"

David scurried out from behind Sharon and said, "Of course, of course. We can sit right here in the lobby, can't we, dear?"

Knutson noticed that their posteriors had barely hit the cushions before Sharon asked, "What about it?"

"Mrs. Hoffman, any time a death occurs, such as that suffered by John Hofstead, it is always necessary to make inquiries. I believe my deputy here explained this to your husband when they came out to collect the snowmobile. But in addition to the question of liability and things that may arise of a legal nature, it is natural for the victim's loved ones, in this case, Mrs. Hofstead, to try to understand what happened. We would just like a better understanding of what happened that night, to see if we can understand why Mr. Hofstead, an experienced snowmobiler, died when and where he did."

Orly noticed that David Hoffman was looking rather pale and nervous. He may have had something to say, but in any event, he was not given the chance. Sharon Hoffman wore that "it's over and don't bother us now" impatient look. It annoyed Knutson that even before he had finished his sentence she was saying, "I'm sure there is nothing that we could tell you that would add anything to what you already know. We were fortunate to be able to have Mr. Hofstead as our guest. He seemed to be a fine man and we regret the accident, but we now have other guests to care for, so…"

Knutson was not about to be dismissed. "Yes, well, I noticed that there was no one around this morning. Do you have guests staying here at the present time?"

"Not at present, but we anticipate a busy weekend."

"Sure," thought Orly, "nothing like one of your guests dying out on a frozen lake to make everyone want to come and spend the weekend." Aloud he said, "I can assure you we won't take up much of your time. The sheriff has never been here before and has not had a chance to meet you. He just wants to see if you can clear up a few things. Right, Sheriff?"

"Yes. You see, when Orly went out to the scene of the accident, he took some photos. I have them here. There's one thing that bothers me." He started passing them, upside down, to David Hoffman. Sharon, however, reached across and grabbed the first picture, a photograph of Hofstead's body under the loon. Knutson sighed inwardly. "At least we have her prints," he thought.

Sharon looked at it quickly, "So? If a picture is worth a thousand words, then this seems to tell the whole story."

"Not exactly," Knutson patiently explained. He took out a second picture and handed it to David. "You see, this is where you

165

found the snowmobile when you went out to retrieve it. Do either of you notice anything different about that?"

"No," David mumbled.

"Of course not," said Sharon, dismissing the question.

"We were concerned about how that snowmobile could have gotten all the way back down to the lake after Hofstead fell off under the loon. Those things aren't supposed to go that far all by themselves, are they? We thought we would like to ask your opinion since Orly tells me that you are quite a snowmobile racer, Mr. Hoffman."

David Hoffman suddenly appeared relaxed and glowed at the flattery. "Well, I don't know about that, but, yeah, I've done my share of snowmobiling, I guess."

"So, do you think this could have happened? That the snowmobile could have traveled fifty feet with no one on it?" asked Knutson, as he handed him another glossy print.

"Hmmmm," mused David. "Normally I'd say no. But apparently it did this time."

"How do you explain that?"

Hoffman furrowed his brow in a deep scowl. "I guess I can't. The accelerator must have stuck. But I'm sure that it has never done that before."

"We checked out the machine. There was no evidence that it could have malfunctioned in that manner."

"It was awfully cold that night. Maybe it froze up or something."

"Well, we'll probably never know," Knutson said lightly. "We just thought that if we could clear it up, Mrs. Hofstead would have the satisfaction of knowing. Tell me, what was his mood that night?"

Sharon jumped in before David could answer. "We hardly knew the man. We spoke to him by telephone, of course, but other than that we only met him a few hours before he died. He seemed perfectly normal to me."

"We were just wondering, you know, if he could have been despondent or ..."

"Oh," David said, with surprise and perhaps relief. "You mean, like, could he have run his sled into the loon as a suicide? I don't know, but now that you mention it, he did look a little worried, didn't he, Sharon? Maybe he did. Yeah, that would explain it. Sure."

"You mean," Palmer asked reasonably, "that would explain what his sled was doing all the way down on the lake?"

Hoffman's face reflected a yo-yoing of emotions. The relieved expression evident only a few seconds before was now replaced by a look of panic. "Er, no," he stuttered. "But it might explain how he happened to hit the loon in the first place, huh?"

"Perhaps." Still looking at David, he continued. "Can you give us a little chronology of what happened that night?"

"Oh, I don't know," Hoffman stuttered. "That was almost a week ago. I don't know if I can remember how things went."

Sharon interrupted again. "I think I can remember quite accurately. The dinner was over at about nine thirty. I remember because we pay the busboy by the hour. It was at that time that he cleaned the last dishes off the table. Mr. Hofstead and the rest had come here to snowmobile and they were determined to do it. Personally, I would have liked for them to just go to bed and wait until it was warmer, but when they pay to go snowmobiling, you have to let them do it. David and I brought appropriate gear into the lobby so they could dress right here. We wanted them to be together because they were not all experienced snowmobilers and we wanted to be sure they were all properly outfitted. Actually, this took only about ten or fifteen minutes, and then David led them to the shed where the sleds are kept. That's about all I can tell you. I didn't think it was necessary for me to wait up. We have a system whereby if any of the guests need anything after hours they can buzz us in our private quarters. I didn't hear anything and after a while, knowing that I had to get up to help serve breakfast to the whole party, I went to bed."

"You must have heard snowmobiles coming and going in the night," Orly interjected.

"I suppose I did, but I didn't really think about that. I thought David was capable of handling it," she said, with a hint of sarcasm in her voice.

"Since he managed to lose one," Knutson added, unkindly, "perhaps he wasn't."

David was insulted. "Just a minute here. I didn't lose anybody. There were six of us. Mr. Swenson and his wife, Mr. Pemmerman, or whatever his name was, Mr. Sandberg, Mr. Hofstead, and myself. We kept together for a while, then I noticed Mr. Sandberg break off and go back to the motel. I saw Mr. Pekerman go off to town and decided he could find his own way back, which apparently he did. The rest of us zoomed around for a while and then I went back to see how things were going and to check on Mr. Sandberg. When I got back on the lake, I could see Swenson and his wife, but I didn't see Mr. Hofstead. But he was the most experienced one of all—I was hardly worried about him. In fact, when I got back, his sled was already in the shed."

This was news. "It was?" asked Knutson, in a voice that did not well conceal the fact that the whole course of the investigation may have been changed. "Why didn't you say anything about this before?"

"Nobody asked me. Why, is it important? When I returned with that young couple, the Sandberg sled and the Polaris that Hofstead was driving were already in the shed. Only the Petterman sled was still out. But so what? I figured he was still in town. Anyway, I heard a sled about one o'clock, and then I heard another one start up maybe half an hour later."

"What were you doing at this time?" Palmer asked.

"I was in the bathroom."

"The whole time?"

"Just about. I came back and I was so cold that I took a hot shower. Then I went into the kitchen and made a cup of hot tea. Then I went back into the bathroom."

"You went back into the bathroom with a cup of tea?" Orly asked, indelicately.

"No, if you must know, I finished the tea in the kitchen before I went back to the bathroom."

Orly was not content to let the matter rest. "Why did you go back to the bathroom?"

"Why do you suppose?"

"Well, you seem to have been there for a long time."

"Yes, ahem, I've, er, been having some problems lately."

Sharon sighed, "It's true, Deputy, he really has."

"And what were you doing all this time, Mrs. Hoffman?" Knutson asked.

"As I said, I was sleeping. I had no idea that anything was wrong until the next morning when poor Mrs. Hofstead couldn't find her husband."

Knutson leaned forward and nonchalantly, but carefully gathered up the pictures and put them back into the envelope. As he rose, he sighed, "I suppose there are some things we will never know. But I appreciate your help. We've got work to do back in town, Orly. We'd best be getting back."

As the door was closed abruptly behind them, a small chunk of snow was dislodged from the roof and with unerring accuracy found Orly's neck. He muttered a vile curse and added acidly, "Some hosts. They couldn't even offer us coffee. I think they must be the murderers."

TWENTY-ONE

PALMER KNUTSON SPENT THE drive back to town in silent contemplation. He thought about Orly's suspicions on the basis of the Hoffman's lack of hospitality. Orly hadn't meant it, of course, but Palmer mused that it would be nice if the Hoffmans, one or both, really had done the murder. They were only transplanted Minnesotans, after all, and not really "one of us." They certainly had the means—it was their machine—and they had the opportunity, at least David did. But as the sheriff tried to concentrate on the problem at hand, the morning concert from Minnesota Public Radio featured Beethoven's Ninth Symphony. One of the things he most appreciated about his Acura Integra was the stereo system. He now turned up the volume and, as he drove through Pelican Rapids, he waved his hand to direct the London Symphony Orchestra and accompanied them with his made-up German.

This amused Orly. A year ago he would have returned to the Law Enforcement Center and told everyone who would listen how silly the sheriff was, and suggest perhaps there should be a change.

Orly had taken German in college and had been forced to learn a little Schiller. Knutson's German bore no resemblance to any language, but Orly knew better than to correct his boss. Instead, he found himself singing along in the correct words which, he decided, were not all that far from what the sheriff was singing. The whole episode had the effect of a catharsis, and Orly was in the mood to do some more work. As they returned to Fergus Falls, he said, "It's only about ten thirty. Why don't we drop these photographs off for the BCA boys and then go over and talk to Clarence Sandberg? We ought to be able to get some coffee there."

"At least," agreed the sheriff.

Clarence and Joey Sandberg lived on the winding Somerset Road on the east side of the city. It was a nice four-bedroom ranch style, painted white with stark black trim. A critic would say that the house had no personality, but in fact, when one got to know the Sandbergs, one would have to agree it reflected the individual dynamics of the owners. Besides keeping the inhabitants warm and dry, what else should a house do?

Joey Sandberg seemed surprised to see them. "Sheriff, and, uh, uh, come in, come in."

"Good morning, Mrs. Sandberg. Have you met my deputy, Orly Peterson?"

Orly extended a hand and he and Joey breathed out their mutual "nice to meet you" in unison. With a puzzled look, she asked, "What can I do for you?"

Palmer twirled his fur cap around in his hand and replied, "Oh, you know, we thought we would just come around and ask about that business with John Hofstead."

Joey's eyebrows pinched together in a manner that suggested a gastric disorder. "There's not a problem, is there?"

"No, no, no, no, nothing like that," Palmer assured her. "We just want to see if we can figure out how it happened, that's all. Being in insurance, I'm sure you can see that."

Joey couldn't see it, but she said, "Of course, of course. Come in and sit down. Let me take your coats. I'll just go and get us some coffee. Clarence is down at the office, but he said he was just going in to check the mail. He'll be home anytime now. Just sit anyplace. I'll be right back."

"Now that's what I call an unlikely murder suspect," Orly muttered, as he leaned back on the sofa and began to skim a *National Geographic*.

True to her word, Joey was right back with a tray of six varieties of cookies. "I had just put the morning coffee in a HotPot. Would you like something with your coffee? Actually, as you can see, they are leftover Christmas cookies, but they've been in the freezer and should be all right. Baking cookies at Christmas time is one of my little weaknesses. I always get carried away and make too many." After a pause she added with false modesty, "But at least you have a choice this way. Now, what can I tell you?"

Palmer and Orly exchanged a conspiratorial glance and began a systematic assault on the cookie tray. The sheriff said, "What can you tell us about that night?"

"Not much. Or, at least, not much that you would find interesting. We were the first ones to get there, I think, although Pek and Iris came about the same time. In fact, they might have been there just a tad before us. Clarence has always liked to be prompt, he enjoys being the first one to arrive at every event, but to tell you the truth, I felt a little silly getting there before the Hofsteads even did. I tried to tell him that before we left, but you know Clarence."

Palmer, who really didn't know Clarence, politely nodded as though he did.

"So anyway, we get there and get shown to our rooms. Then we got together and had supper, and then the boys, and that Swenson woman—or Nelson, I guess it is—went out snowmobiling, and that was the last time I ever saw poor John alive. We didn't know anything about it until the next morning."

Palmer arched a friendly eyebrow and asked, "And you didn't feel like going snowmobiling?"

"Do you have any idea how cold it was that night? No one should have been out there. I told Clarence that, too. I said, 'It's too cold out there, Clarence.' But you know Clarence." Again Knutson nodded, but belied his knowledge of Clarence when he asked, "Did he do this sort of thing often?"

"Clarence? Of course not. He had never been on a snowmobile in his life. He doesn't like the cold, you know. He likes his TV and his basement workshop, does Clarence. But he wanted to show John that the company would go on just as before with him as president. To tell you the truth, he did surprise me a little that night, by going out in the cold, I mean, but as he said, 'It's my responsibility to keep open the lines of communication with other members of the company, now that John's retiring.' I still thought it was a dumb thing to do, but I sort of admired him for it."

Palmer leaned forward, sipped his coffee, and selected a piece of chocolate shortbread. "So he was certain he was going to be asked to head the company?"

"Well, of course he was. There was nobody else, really, although he worried that Young Gary and his computer might be some competition. In fact, when John didn't turn up for breakfast, everybody started worrying that he was meeting with Gary Swenson to discuss the future." She paused and made a rather grotesque smile. "Guess not, huh?"

"And what did you do when Clarence was out snowmobiling?"

"Me? I stayed in my room, naturally. Where else would I go? I just watched *The Tonight Show*. I like Leno better than that other guy, you know, the guy with the gap in his teeth."

Knutson, who was a Letterman fan, decided to let it pass. "And you were there when Clarence came in?"

"Certainly. To tell you the truth, I had got ready for bed and was watching Leno with only one eye. I may have fallen asleep before he got in."

"But you remember speaking to your husband when he returned?"

"Yes. Or at least, I think I do. I can sometimes be pretty groggy when I fall asleep like that."

"What does Clarence anticipate happening now?" Orly asked, whose inside knowledge of who the president would be created a rather morbid curiosity about the losers.

"Well, it will be up to Martha, I suppose, since she inherits the company—at least, I presume she does. They're going to have a meeting on Friday to sort things out, but Clarence is assuming he'll be asked to take over."

Palmer gave his deputy a disgusted look to indicate that he should stick to the subject and, turning back to Joey, asked, "That night, when you had that meal together, did John seem all right?"

"Far as I could tell. I never thought about it, anyway. But say, now that you mention it, when I look back on it, I don't remember him being involved too much. He is usually the one leading toasts and things like that. Hmm. Yah, I bet there was something wrong."

A noise came from the back room and a current of cold air passed along the floor. "That's Clarence now," added Joey, unnecessarily. "Clarence, come into the living room. We've got company."

They heard Clarence peel off his rubber boots and amble into the kitchen. He came into the living room with an empty mug and a cheery, "So you got some coffee in here, then? Oh. Hello, Sheriff. It there something wrong?"

"No, no. Orly and I are just looking into the Hofstead tragedy." Palmer had long discovered that few people really questioned the motives of the sheriff, but since the line had worked so well before he added, "But as an insurance man, you can understand why we have to look into these matters."

Clarence, of course, didn't understand any more than his wife had, but he also nodded and said, "Of course. Er, how can I help?" He lowered his massive rear end into a protesting chair and added, "Fine man, John. A fine man."

Palmer nodded and said, "Well, your wife has been most helpful already. She told us how you arrived and about the dinner and everything. But just as you came in, she decided that Mr. Hofstead appeared to be somewhat distracted that night. Do you agree?"

"Distracted?" He looked up at his wife. "What do you mean, 'distracted'?"

"I guess I didn't really say, 'distracted,' that's the sheriff's word. But it fits. Yes, that's it. 'Distracted.'" Orly looked at Knutson with a superciliously raised eyebrow as if to say "Who is it who always warns against putting words into the mouths of witnesses?" Joey nodded and nervously rubbed her index finger into her palm. "Now, don't you think that describes John that night? You know how he always liked to be the man who is always conspicuously in charge? He wasn't on that night, was he?"

Clarence considered this and replied, "Now that you mention it, no, I don't think he was his usual self. I remember thinking that at the time. But you know what I thought it was? I thought he was looking us all over. Like he still hadn't made up his mind who he wanted for the next president. I remember not liking the feeling."

"But, as far as either of you can remember," the sheriff continued, "did he say anything out of the ordinary?"

"Not that I can recall," answered Joey. "But hey, I put another pot on when you came in. It should be ready by now. I'll be right back."

"I can't recall him saying anything out of the ordinary either," Clarence added, as he smiled approvingly at his wife's hospitality. "Besides, I only felt that way during that dinner. Afterwards, when we were going snowmobiling, he seemed in fine spirits. But that was John, of course. He loved snowmobiling."

"And you didn't?" Knutson prompted.

"Well, I'd never done it before. To tell you the truth, I've never had an urge to do it. Joey, now, Joey even knows how to run one of those machines. A few years ago, when the girls were still in high school, we went out to Joey's sister's place. They live out by Perham. Anyway, those people had just bought a snowmobile and Joey and the girls all went out and had a good time. I would have gone, too, I suppose, but I was just getting over the flu and still felt lousy. But you know something? I think I sort of missed out. Once I got the hang of that thing the other night, I had a pretty good time. I would have enjoyed it even more if it hadn't been so cold. It didn't seem to bother anybody else, but I thought it was colder than a banker's heart. I just said 'the heck with it' after a while and went back to the Otter Slide."

"So you were the first one to return? Was Hofstead still out there?"

"Yah, I was the first one back, so John must have been out there. I don't know. I didn't really think about it. I just wanted to get back and get warm."

"Did you go back out again?" Orly asked innocently.

"What? Of course I didn't. I went straight to bed. And I tell you, after zooming around out there in that cold air, I slept sounder than a drunken Swedish lumberjack!"

"So you didn't hear when the others came back?"

"I wouldn't have heard them if they had ridden through my room."

Joey returned, bustling in with a new pot of steaming coffee. Both Palmer and Orly were sated, but decided since Joey had gone to the trouble to make it, they should have one more small cup. There seemed to be no point in rehashing the night at the Otter Slide anymore, so Knutson and the Sandbergs compared experiences of having college-age daughters. Orly, who also had a considerable interest in college girls, had sense enough to keep his thoughts to himself.

The sheriff and his deputy lunched at Hardee's. It was not a memorable lunch, a fact which owed more to the consumption of an excess of cookies than it did to the quality of the hamburger. They munched in silence while skimming a borrowed *Star Tribune*. Finally, Orly said, "So, what about the Sandbergs?"

Knutson grunted, "So what about them?"

"How do you see them in all this?"

"What kind of sentence is that?"

"I mean, I suppose, do you think they could have bumped off Hofstead?"

"Could have, I guess," Palmer admitted, wiping ketchup off his chin. "They were there."

"All right, let me put it another way. Do you think they killed him?"

"Do you?"

"I asked you first."

"Okay, fair enough. What do we know about them? They were there. Clarence was a longtime employee and by all accounts a loyal dog. If he found he would be passed over, would he be angry? I would guess so. Mrs. Sandberg? Wanting her husband to climb to the top? Social pretensions? Not as likely, I would say. She doesn't seem the type, but who knows? There is one thing that I think we should find out, although it may take a while. Just what were the finances of the company? If, for instance, Sandberg had been involved in a little financial sleight of hand, the installation of a new president would involve a new audit that could potentially destroy him. The same thing, of course, would hold true for anyone in the company who might have been on the fiddle. But the Sandbergs especially might be susceptible to money pressures. It takes a lot of money to keep two girls in private colleges, and they're not the kind of people who want to descend the social ladder. So bottom line, yes, either of them could have done it, but both seem unlikely killers. What do you think?"

Orly had been generally nodding as Knutson had reviewed the case against the Sandbergs. "Yah, I basically agree. I did find it interesting that once again we had a case of where either one of them could have actually done the murder. They both had the means and opportunity. Clarence had just learned to ride a snowmobile, but it's not like learning to pilot a jet fighter. Do it for twenty minutes and you can essentially do it for the rest of your life. Don't tell that proud little David Hoffman I said that! So now we also find out that Mrs. Sandberg had also operated one of those things. Neither can claim with absolute certainty what the other was doing, and in any event, their only alibis are each other's. In fact, it could be that they did it together. The couple that murders together, stays together! And you know something, maybe it was just the jolt of caffeine, but I thought they seemed to be getting a little antsy by the time we left. On the other hand, sometimes you just gotta follow your gut, and I just can't see them as murderers. When are we going to see the Pekanens?"

"I spoke to Mrs. Pekanen—Iris, is it?—on the phone yesterday, and she suggested that we come by about one thirty. That would give us time to talk before their kids came home from school. Since they've got three of them, I thought that was a real good idea."

"What about the husband?"

"She said that she was sure he could arrange to be there, too. Can you face being charming for a while longer today?"

"But of course," replied Orly, putting his stocking cap at a rakish angle.

Iris Pekanen met them at the door. She was wearing an overlarge sweater in an unsuccessful attempt to disguise her lumpish figure. As she stuck her head out of the door to greet them, her large eyeglasses fogged up, and as she turned to show them in to the entry, she bumped into a straw Christmas decoration that was still hanging on her closet door. Knutson and Peterson were both somehow able to hide their amusement behind a facade of concern.

"Are you all right?" the sheriff asked.

"Yes, yes. Certainly. Give me a minute to clean these things off. Pek?" she yelled, "Pek? The sheriff is here."

Myron Pekanen ambled lazily into the living room as Iris abruptly left to clean her glasses. Pek sat down on what was obviously his favorite chair, motioned toward the sofa, and said, "Sit down. Take off your coats and stay a while."

Since he made no effort to take their coats, Knutson and Peterson took the initiative of laying them on an unused living room chair and sat where their host had indicated. Pek looked up at them from under his puffy eyebrows and said, "What's up?"

Knutson started to go into his by now familiar routine about clearing up the events surrounding the death of John Hofstead. Pekanen, however, was not as docile as the others and challenged the benign assurance the sheriff was offering. "No, just because I sell insurance doesn't mean I see what you need to look into that for. The guy died in an accident. You investigated it at the time and now you're looking into it all over again. What's the poop?"

Orly jumped in. "You see, all of a sudden there is a question of liability. We've found out that Hofstead was a pretty good snowmobiler and now maybe there might be an issue of whether the machine was poorly designed or perhaps maintained improperly."

"Lawsuits, again, huh? Let me tell you something. We got to do something about those lawyers. Every time somebody gets a nosebleed they are looking around to blame somebody. I was once threatened with a lawsuit because some guy claimed I failed to sell him enough hail insurance. Can you believe it? We sell 'em everything we can. But this guy wanted to sue, claiming that I had not done my job sufficiently and that left him underinsured. One of my kids says he wants to be a lawyer when he grows up. I say, having an insurance salesman and a lawyer in the same family is more than our reputation could stand." Pek roared at his own wit.

"Well, anyway," Knutson cut in, "we've talked to some of the others who were there that night, and we just wanted to see if you could add anything."

"Okay, there's not much to tell. We went out there and got there about the same time as the Sandbergs. That's a switch. Clarence always has to be the first one wherever he goes. So anyway, we get there. I go down to have a snort before supper, then we eat, then we all go snowmobiling. I didn't know anything was wrong until the next morning. I don't see where I can help you with anything."

"Had you ever been there before?" Orly asked.

Pek leaned out to see where Iris was. "Well, yah, I was out there a couple of times last summer for some beers with a client. But, you see, I sort of fibbed to Iris about it because she was getting on me about my drinking. But yah, I'd met both the Hoffmans before. Didn't really talk to them much or get to know them, you know, but at least I knew who they were."

"So you knew your way around there?"

"Sure, why?"

"Just asking, that's all," Orly obscurely replied. "You knew how to run a snowmobile before that night?"

"Of course, who doesn't?"

Ignoring the question, Knutson asked, "Did Hofstead seem like the kind of snowmobile driver who would have an accident like that?"

"Nope. John knew what he as doing, he always did. But that's one thing you see in the insurance business. You can see the greatest stock car racer go through a red light or drive off and hit a tree. I was just reading about this college all-American football player who broke his ankle when he stepped on a walnut. You just never know. That's what I always tell people. You just never know!"

Iris came in carrying four mugs, managing to get her finger inside each one. "Coffee everyone?"

Everyone muttered their assent and Iris returned with a pot of coffee and a plate of thickly buttered banana bread. Knutson and Peterson did their civic duty.

"Now that both of you are here, there are a couple of questions I'd like you both to think about. It has been suggested that John Hofstead seemed a little distracted at the dinner that night. Would you agree?"

"I don't know," Pek replied, licking the butter off of his thumb. "Seemed pretty normal to me. I was going to see if I could have a little private talk with him, but I never got the chance. I wasn't sitting real close to him at supper. You notice anything, Iris?"

Iris, delighted to have been asked, took her time in answering. She finished her second piece of banana bread before she said, "You know, I think maybe he was. John had this laugh that seemed to cut right through whatever noise there was around. It was a great laugh, and when you heard it you couldn't help smiling yourself. But you know—and I never really thought about it until now—I don't remember hearing that laugh."

Knutson continued, "Did either of you notice a certain amount of tension surrounding the weekend because of the issue of Hofstead's retirement and the choosing of his successor?"

"Oh, yah," Pek blurted, "was there ever! You shoulda seen the way Clarence looked at Swenson whenever 'Young Gary' oozed his way alongside of Hofstead. I got the impression that Clarence was mostly upset that Swenson was always beating him to it. And of course, each wife snubbed the other. Even Borghild looked a little uptight. The only one who didn't was Harry Kvamme. He just sat there looking bored or confused, I couldn't decide which. Maybe he couldn't either."

"What about you?"

"Me?"

"Yah, were you 'uptight' about the weekend?"

"Nah! 'Course, I had a little relaxant along with me. But nah, nobody ever took me seriously anyway. I know they don't see me as executive material. They know I can sell policies, though, so they won't get rid of me. I once thought that I might be Hofstead's 'compromise candidate,' so to speak. I mean, if you hire Gary, you infuriate Clarence, and if you hire Clarence, you sour Gary. If you hire me, both of them resent it, but they still stay with the company and Hofstead can sit back and still enjoy a profitable business. It made a lot of sense. Too much sense, I suppose. Now I don't know if we'll ever find out who he wanted. We're going to have this big meeting on Friday, and I suppose Martha will tell us who she wants."

"Tell us what happened when you went off snowmobiling."

"There isn't all that much to tell. It was me and Clarence and John and Gary—the last ride of the big four, so to speak—and Gary's wife and that Hoffman guy. We just went around the lake for a while and then I got cold so I went into Vergas for a little something to warm the blood."

"What time did you return to the Otter Slide?" Knutson asked.

Orly noticed the intense anger in Iris's face as she waited for her husband to reply. "Well, I guess we sort of closed the place down," Pek replied, with a guilty glance at Iris. "I suppose it was about one o'clock when I left."

"Did you see any other snowmobiles? Did you notice anybody at the Otter Slide?"

"I don't remember. There might have been another sled on the lake. Seems to me I saw a light and I wondered if that could be one of us. But then, from a distance it's sort of hard to tell if it's a snowmobile headlight or just somebody's yard light on the shore, especially if you're moving. When I got back to the resort, I didn't see anybody. But there were still some lights on. There was still a light on in the shed, and the lobby light was on, of course, and there were some of the room lights on. I know, because I tried to figure out which lights belonged to our room and I was wondering if Iris was still up waiting for me."

"Were you, Iris?" Palmer asked.

"Of course not. I went to bed right after Pek left. I went to sleep and didn't awaken until the morning."

Pek blurted out, "Are you sure? I thought I remembered you getting up and leaving the room for a while."

"Certainly not," she replied acidly. "Besides, you were hardly in a condition to remember anything."

Knutson gently brought them around to the events of the morning. "Were you concerned when Hofstead didn't show up for breakfast?"

"Not at first," Pek answered. "It was only later, you know, when Martha started getting real anxious, that the rest of us started thinking something was wrong. We were all thinking he had gone off with Swenson, so when they came in without Hofstead, well, then something seemed wrong."

"Did anybody else seem especially worried?"

"Why are you asking a question like that? Are you implying that somebody's personally liable for his death? If you are, well, I gotta admit that, yah, David Hoffman looked real worried. His wife kept trying to calm him down so they could get breakfast on the table. Look, uh, I'll stay and talk with you guys as long as you like, but I do have an appointment this afternoon, and uh…"

"No, no. We're about done, I guess," Knutson replied. "Orly, do you have anything further?"

"No, except to tell Mrs. Pekanen that this is really wonderful banana bread. Thank you so much."

Iris blushed with pride, "Oh, you're so welcome."

Back at the sheriff's office, a fax was waiting from the Polk County, Iowa, sheriff's office. It read:

Palmer. Your deputy called the Des Moines police to inquire about one Laura Epperly. Somehow that got shuttled over to us at the sheriff's office. Laura Epperly was born in 1968 to Alan and Linda Meland of Iowa City, Iowa. The father was killed a year later in Vietnam. The mother was an assistant librarian at the University of Iowa who was killed by a bomb placed by a radical group in 1970. The little girl was apparently taken in by an aunt in Des Moines. Records show that she married a Thomas Epperly in June of last year. We could find no violations on her driving record and no other data of any kind. Sorry we couldn't be of more help. If you need more data, please inform us of the nature and purpose of your inquiry.

Are you going to show me some good fishing this summer?

David Nelson
Sheriff

TWENTY-TWO

"Is Swenson going up to his office just to meet us? How come he wouldn't see us in his home?" asked Orly Peterson the next morning as they drove the short distance to the Kaddatz building in downtown Fergus Falls.

"According to him," replied Palmer Knutson, with obvious distaste, "it is because he would be close to his computer in case he needed to refer to it. I can't think of one thing that a computer could do to help us in this case. By the way, what do you think of that information we got from Iowa?"

"Laura Meland, you mean? I might point out, by the way, that they probably got most of the information that they sent on her from computerized files," Orly answered, and as the sheriff looked up sourly, added, "uh, no offense. Anyway, we've been looking for a Laura Epperly. Maybe we should run Laura Meland by everyone again."

"I already did that. I stopped by to see Mrs. Hofstead last night. I've solved the riddle of Laura Epperly."

"Perhaps you would be so kind as to share it with me," Orly said, testily.

"Yah, it's an interesting story. It seems John Hofstead went down to the University of Iowa back in 1970 for some kind of actuarial conference. Well, you know how things were then—actually, you don't, because you're so disgustingly young—but anyhow, there was a lot of student radicalism. That was about the time that a group called 'The Weathermen' had everybody shaking in their boots. So Hofstead has been pretty well insulated from that sort of stuff and it's all a big shock to him. One night he goes down to the library at the university and this guy runs into him. They both go sprawling and as Hofstead is doing his best to apologize, there is a big explosion in the library and the guy streaks off. It turns out that somebody set off a bomb in the library and a librarian was killed. John didn't know this at the time, of course, but the next day he reads about the death and how everybody is looking for a man last seen running from the library. Hofstead immediately thinks he has seen the murderer. He goes down to the police to describe him. According to Martha, Hofstead described him as having long hair and a beard. That description covered about seventy percent of the male population of Iowa City in 1970, and they never found the guy. Well, John is remorseful. He figures he had the murderer on the ground and he let him get away. Then he reads about the victim. She had a little girl, the father had died in Vietnam—sad story. Hofstead feels somehow responsible and, since he is in the insurance business, he buys a small life insurance policy for the girl."

Knutson parked on the street and shut off the engine. He nodded his head in the direction of the late insurance man's building and said, "All in all, a classy thing for him to do. He never even met the girl. You could see how proud of him Martha was while she was telling the story." The sheriff paused and whispered, almost to himself, "I want to get the murderer, Orly, and the sooner the better. Let's see what Swenson can tell us."

Borghild was still seated at her secretary's desk. She looked like the proverbial cat that swallowed the canary as she said over the intercom, "The sheriff and his deputy are here to see you, Gary. Shall I send them in?" Knutson and Peterson, who knew her secret and knew that she was relishing her last day as a secretary, smiled conspiratorially.

Young Gary was effervescent. "Come in, come in. Hey, Borghild, is there any coffee for these guys? Sit down, sheriff and, uh ..."

"Orly Peterson."

"Yes, Orly," resumed Swenson in his best informal and ingratiating manner. "Now, it's about John, isn't it? Such a tragedy. It's my fault, you know. I blame myself. I really do. I should have stayed with him. But how was I supposed to know he would go out again?"

Knutson, who was certain that Swenson did not really blame himself, was content to mumble, "Of course, who knew? That was a surprise, then? I mean, that he went out a second time?"

"Oh, yes. I thought we were all done for the night. When we got back to the resort, Faye Janice and I just said good night and went straight to our room."

"Let's go back to earlier in the evening," Knutson began.

"Why?" Swenson interrupted. "You're just investigating the accident, aren't you?"

"Well, yes," the sheriff continued evasively, "but we want to understand not only how it happened, but why."

"I see," said Swenson, who didn't.

"Now, when did you first see Mr. Hofstead that night?"

"Actually, we arrived at the resort together, or, I should say, at the same time."

"And did you notice anything at all different about him? That is, did he seem moody or depressed?"

"John? Of course not. John was never depressed. To tell you the truth, though, when we met in the lobby of the resort, he seemed, well, not glad to see me. I guess I was expecting him to be a little more enthusiastic about the weekend."

"Would you say he seemed 'distracted'?" Orly ventured.

"'Distracted?' Yeah, that's it. He seemed sort of distracted. I suppose you know why we had all gone there. John was going to pick one of us to be the new president of the company. Funny, now that I think of it. I remember saying to Faye Janice that John looked a little uncomfortable, and I commented something about how he looked like he was going to give me the bad news. Later, though, after dinner, he seemed cheery enough. We all had a fine time snowmobiling. I'm sure he was cheery then. Say, you're not suggesting that he drove that sled into the loon on purpose are you? I don't believe it. John was not the sort to commit suicide. On the other hand, he was making a profound change in his life, and I'm sure it wouldn't be easy to give up what you had spent your life doing and ..."

Palmer let him ramble on about a man's work defining him before he interrupted with, "So the company was in good shape, then?"

This was a question Swenson had been waiting for. "Just look!" He leaned forward and typed various commands on his computer.

In seconds the sheriff was treated to an awesome display of actuarial science, combined with Swenson's vision for the company. It was with difficulty that Knutson asked, "Did you get an indication of who Hofstead would ask to head the company?"

Swenson paused for a while before saying, "Not actually, no. I did get the feeling that night, however, that it wasn't going to be me. I felt that he was being extra kind and friendly on that snowmobiling ride because he was going to tell me he had picked Clarence to head the company."

"Would you have stayed with Clarence as president?"

"Probably. He isn't so bad, I guess, and the main thing is that he is pretty long in the tooth himself. But I would have looked around, all the same."

"What about if Mr. Pekanen were chosen?"

"Not likely, but if that were the case, then I definitely would leave. Don't get me wrong, he knows the business. He once told me that he even used to go down to the University of Iowa every summer for their actuarial seminars. He claims to be only a few credits short of a master's degree and that the only reason he doesn't have it is because of the wife and kids. I mean, you'd hardly think it from talking to him, but he was sort of a hippy once. Actually, I think the real reason was because he didn't like to wear shoes. But really, you know, I don't think I would like working for him."

"So now that Mrs. Hofstead has to take charge," Orly asked, "who do you think will be the new president?"

"I'm sure I can't say," Swenson said, beaming with confidence. "I did take some time to prepare a memo on the direction of the company, however, and hope that she has a chance to read it by the time we meet tomorrow."

"If I could just clear up a couple of points regarding that late-night snowmobile ride," said Palmer, trying to get the interview back on course. "Did you all go off in one party?"

"Yes, I'm sure we did."

"And then what happened?"

"I did want to get a moment with John, just to say a few things about the company, so I stuck with him almost all of the time. I noticed that one of the sleds returned rather soon. That may have been Clarence, because I didn't see him much at all. Then I noticed we were down to four, and when that Hoffman guy told us he was returning to the resort it was just John, Faye Janice, and myself. As I said, we returned together and separated and that was the last time I saw him alive."

"What did he say as you left him?"

"Near as I can remember, he said 'good night.'"

"And in the morning?" the sheriff prompted.

"We didn't see anybody. Faye Janice and I went cross-country skiing in the woods before breakfast. It's beautiful at that time of day, you know, even if it is beastly cold. Anyway, we didn't hear about John until we came in for breakfast."

"Yes, well, John Hofstead will be missed, that's for sure," Palmer added, as a way of noting that there was little more to be said about it. "By the way, since your wife was also out there, we'd like to ask her if she noticed anything. When would be the best time to talk to her?"

"She has a couple of phy ed classes up at the university this morning, but she's done by ten thirty and then she has office hours until noon. Maybe you would like to talk to her over there."

"Yah, sounds good," said the sheriff, as he stood up and began to put on his coat. "And Borghild," he added with a wink as they made their way out. "Thanks for the coffee."

Faye Janice Nelson had her office in the newly renamed Gherkin Memorial Field House. Her eight-thirty class, "Aerobics for Life," was a popular choice among the sorority set, and her nine-thirty class, "Aerobics for Life II," was a natural sequel. Basically, the upper division class used a different tape—Faye Janice did not like to burden herself with class preparations. Nonetheless, she did keep her office hours, on the off chance that one of her students would care to stop in and discuss the classes. It was a good time to catch up on her reading.

Palmer Knutson and Orly Peterson were both graduates of Fergus Falls State University. Palmer, of course, had been there as a member of a different generation than Orly. As they walked through the halls of the field house, Palmer reminded his younger colleague of college life of earlier days. "None of this stuff was here, then, you know. I mean, we had the old gym and everybody thought that was fine. Of course, there wasn't anything too special about being an athlete then. They got a little special treatment, in that they were given cushy jobs officiating intramural games and things like that, but nothing like this. Look here—weight room! When I went here there were a couple of barbells and some dumbbells in the corner of the locker room. Look at that stuff—machines to remake the human body. Why don't they just do push-ups?"

Orly, who regularly worked out on a Nautilus, said nothing.

"And look at this," Knutson continued. "'Football video room!'— gimme a break. Now I grant you that Francis Olson is a pretty good coach, but this is ridiculous. Those pampered guys even have their own training table. And these offices! When you think of what those poor saps who teach English and history have to put up with, it makes you sick. Well, maybe the new president can 'reprioritize,' as they say in the ed-biz."

They passed the offices toward the rear of the building, which were arranged in a descending order of importance and a corresponding descent in size. At the very end were the offices of part-time instructors. Here Faye Janice Nelson had left her door invitingly open. Knutson stuck his head in the doorway and Faye Janice peered at him over the top of her Danielle Steele. "May I help you?" she asked politely.

"Good morning, Ms. Nelson. I'm Palmer Knutson? Otter Tail County Sheriff?" he began, in that annoying way of ending each sentence with a question mark, a habit he had been trying unsuccessfully to get his son to break. "This is my deputy, Orly Peterson."

"Oh, of course, Sheriff. I, er, won't you come in? Is there something the matter?"

"No, nothing to worry about. We were just talking to your husband and …"

"What's wrong with Gary?" she gasped anxiously.

"Nothing is wrong with him," Palmer hastily assured her. "We just wanted to talk to him about what he remembered about last weekend at that resort where John Hofstead died. You know, just some general follow-up questions. And he told us what he could recall about the evening and we just thought since you were there as well, you might be able to add something."

"Oh, I see," said Faye Janice, now too relieved to question the motives behind this kind of investigation into a routine accident.

"Well, what do you want to know? I'm sorry I have such a small office, there's hardly enough room for the couch, but please, make yourselves comfortable."

Knutson lowered himself down on the new modern sofa and remembered the cramped room with broken furniture that served as the office for FFSU's most famous scholar, history professor Harold Winston. As he sat down, he felt a ballpoint pen that he had carelessly left in his pocket poke a hole in the fabric. This gave him a perverse pleasure. "As I understand it, you were all going there as sort of last attempt to influence Hofstead as to whom he should pick as the new president."

"Who told you that?" Faye Janice indignantly replied. "It was a retreat. Other companies do that sort of thing all the time. Mr. Hofstead just wanted everybody to get to know one another better. I'm sure that he would have made his choice based on what was good for the company and on no other basis."

"And do you think that would have been your husband?" Orly asked.

"Of course. But I hardly think that is any of your business."

"Just asking," Orly meekly responded.

"So you all get together at the Otter Slide," continued Knutson, "—and I'm asking you this because as an outsider you could perhaps observe things better than one who worked in the company— did anything strike you as unusual? Was Mr. Hofstead all right? Did he seem his usual self? Was he preoccupied with something?"

This type of appeal to the vanity of a witness was seldom without fruit. Faye Janice considered the question, pouting out her little mouth and passing a finger through her short hair. "Of course, I didn't know Mr. Hofstead as well as some of the others. But when we got there I noticed Gary trying to put on the old super salesman charm act. It always works, I might add. But this time Hofstead seemed oblivious to it. I was wondering if this was a bad sign. We just sort of stood around in that lobby waiting for our keys and I thought it got uncomfortable. Other than that, he seemed to be all right, I guess. I don't know. What did Gary say?"

"Do you like your job?" Knutson abruptly avoided the question and changed the topic.

"Do I like my job? Sure, I suppose. It doesn't pay all that much, but it keeps me in shape. Why?"

"Did Gary like his job?"

"I suppose so. At least, he thought it was a good place to start."

"But both of you were really looking forward to this presidency thing, weren't you? Sort of the next step up on the ladder of success? It was quite an opportunity for him, wasn't it?"

Unaware that the interview had drifted into a much more personal area, Faye Janice looked away and nodded. "Yes, Gary would have done anything to have gotten that position. Now, I don't know. Mrs. Hofstead will probably have that dreadful Sandberg take it over. Funny, but I was even dreaming about quitting this and opening my own little exercise and tanning studio. Now? Who knows?"

"Did you ever get a chance to talk to Mr. Hofstead that night?"

"Not really. I exchanged a few pleasant words with him at dinner that evening. Gary always talked about how Hofstead was such a life of the party. 'He fills the room with a pink glow' was how he put it. I sure didn't see much of that. I thought he was kind of boring."

"What about that evening, when you went snowmobiling?"

"Ah, he seemed to change. You know, I really respect a man, especially one his age, who is willing to go out in the cold and do what he did. I could tell, for instance, that the last place Clarence wanted to be was out on a snowmobile. But Mr. Hofstead really seemed to be enjoying himself. That guy who ran the place—Hoffman, wasn't it?—thought that he had to show everybody what to do. But Mr. Hofstead just sort of took charge and determined what to do and where to go. It was fun just trying to keep up with him."

"What happened when you came back to the resort that night?"

"Actually, there were only the three of us—Gary, Mr. Hofstead, and myself—left out on the lake. Nothing much happened when we returned. Gary and I were together the whole time. We parked our sleds together and went to our room together and got up together. I'm sure I can't add anything to what Gary has told you."

"Did you hear anything later in the night?"

"Such as?"

"Another snowmobile starting up?"

"Gary and I are both sound sleepers."

"What about in the morning?"

"Again, what can I add?" she said, a note of exasperation coming into her voice. "We went for a walk before breakfast together and when we came in to eat everybody was wondering what had happened to Mr. Hofstead."

The sheriff started to stand as he said, "I don't think we have any more questions, Mrs. Swenson—I mean, Ms. Nelson. We've taken up enough of your time. Besides, I think you have a student waiting for you out in the hall."

"I do?" she responded in a shocked voice.

As Knutson and Peterson walked down the hall, a student leaned into Ms. Nelson's office and said, "I want to sign up for field hockey in the spring. Are you Mrs. Ryan?"

It was lunchtime. "You want to eat lunch on campus?" Orly asked.

To Palmer, who recalled what lunch was like on campus in 1968, the offer was less than enticing. "Are you kidding?"

"No. You can get anything you want, from sandwiches to tacos or pizza. They even got a Subway franchise. It's a great place to eat."

Tacos and pizza at the college cafeteria? It was too much! "Yah, okay, why not? I'll just call the office to tell them where we are."

Knutson, who had, as usual, left his cell phone at a place indeterminate, and rejecting as a matter of principle the pay phone in the hall, ducked into the luxurious office of the football coach. Flashing his badge, he said, "Can I use your phone?" That request had never been refused. Orly watched his face from the other side of the glass windows that sealed the football suite off from the rest of the field house. He noticed a sudden change of expression and a rapid turn of the head.

When the sheriff came back he said, "Change of plans. We're going right back to the office. The Bureau of Criminal Apprehension just called. They have a make on those fingerprints. It appears the case has been solved for us."

TWENTY-THREE

NECESSITY CAN SOMETIMES BE the mother of indigestion. It was necessary to change plans. Instead of the culinary delights of the Flying Falcon Food Factory, lunch consisted of a bag of concentrated fat and cholesterol shoved through the car window at Hardee's. It was consumed without interest or enjoyment back at the office where Knutson and Peterson read the fax from the Bureau of Criminal Apprehension. Within minutes they were on their way to make an arrest in the murder of John Hofstead.

The day seemed too bright and cheery for an arrest, the probable outcome of which would be the eventual sentencing of an individual to spend the rest of his life in the state prison near Stillwater. The sun sparkled off the snow in dazzling whiteness, giving Peterson the opportunity to wear his prized California Highway Patrol sunglasses, which were virtually identical to the LAPD sunglasses that he favored in the summer. The California Highway Patrol, however, rarely used them to ward off snow blindness. The only real color in the landscape came from an occasional red barn;

otherwise, squinted eyes were required to distinguish between the light blue of the sky, the light blue of clear ice on the lake, and snow covering the gray branches of the leafless trees. It was only about twelve degrees above zero, but there was no wind. In other words, were it not for the purpose of the visit, it would have been a perfect day to visit the Otter Slide.

Orly was delighted that the BCA report seemed to have removed all doubt as to the murderer. He had possessed a few uneasy suspicions about some people he had grown to like. At least here was a person who wasn't quite "one of us." "I told you, didn't I, that he was the murderer. Only a murderer would not offer someone coffee on a cold winter morning."

Palmer, although recognizing that Orly was not serious, failed to find either humor or satisfaction in the situation. Instead, he inhaled in a kind of curious gasp and affirmed, "Yes, I guess you did."

"What's the matter, aren't you satisfied? Not only have you solved one murder, but it appears that you have solved two. That ought to appeal to the voters of Otter Tail County. And best of all, the evidence is overwhelming and it's somebody hardly anybody knows. What more could you want?"

Palmer took off his fur hat and laid it on the dashboard so he could scratch his head. "I suppose you're right, but the guy just didn't seem like a killer."

"You, of all people, can start talking like that? Remember the Gherkin murder?"

"I know, but you just get a feeling sometimes, and it seems almost illogical when it is so totally wrong. Then, too, I suppose the whole thing is a little anti-climatic because it wasn't really anything we did, it was just a fluke match from a computer."

"What do you mean, 'nothing we did'? If it wasn't for you, Hofstead's death would have been treated as an accident and a double murderer would be free to kill again. Besides, who got the data to put into the computer?"

Palmer grinned. "Yah! You bet! You're right. We did do good, didn't we! Thanks, Orly." But it was an artificial enthusiasm, and Palmer asked, "So, do you want to make the arrest?"

"Nope, that's all yours. But I will read him his Miranda rights if you like."

The sheriff agreed, and in silence they headed out of Vergas, by the quiet and innocent loon, and continued on to the Otter Slide. As they entered the resort, David Hoffman looked up at them as if he had been expecting them. He showed little surprise or emotion as Knutson informed him that he was under arrest on suspicion of first-degree murder. If anything, he looked relieved and barely listened to Peterson's caution that he had the right to remain silent and to consult an attorney. In fact, as soon as the deputy finished the Miranda, Hoffman said, "Yes, of course. May I tell my wife? And, oh yes, may I gather a few personal items to take with me? I assume bail for such a charge is practically out of the question."

Nonplused by his calmness, Knutson said, "Of course we will let you say goodbye to your wife. However, we prefer that you ask her to gather any personal items that you may require. And although I do not doubt your intention to cooperate, I'm afraid that I will have to ask my deputy to use prudent restraints. Orly, your cuffs?"

Hoffman meekly held out his hands to accept the cold steel bands. Orly snapped them in place as Knutson went over to the door that communicated with the Hoffman's private residence, knocked, and called, "Mrs. Hoffman? May we see you for a few minutes?"

Sharon Hoffman entered, looking stern and in control. Her hair was tightly pulled back and she showed no sign of makeup. As she looked from the cuffs on her husband's hands, up to his face, and over to meet the eyes of the two officers, her expression did not change. At last she said, "Would you care to tell me what this is all about?"

Knutson matched her stony expression and said, "I have just placed your husband under arrest for the murder of John Hofstead."

"John Hofstead?" David Hoffman cried, and then fell silent. He looked up at his wife with a confused and pathetic expression.

"I'm sorry, Mrs. Hoffman. If you could just gather a few things for him—toothbrush and other personal items that he may need—we will be on our way."

Orly had been expecting a scene. Instead, he had to suffer a long and bitter stare, and a curt, "Certainly. I'll be right back." Within moments she had placed a small overnight bag in Peterson's hand, mumbled some reassuring words to her husband about the best possible representation, and gave him a rather fierce kiss on the mouth. David Hoffman looked back in a state of total bewilderment. She abruptly left the room, to return in five seconds with her husband's parka. Orly took it and held it out to Hoffman, then gazed at the handcuffs in momentary confusion.

"For heaven's sake!" Palmer snapped. "Take off the cuffs so he can get his coat on."

On their return to Fergus Falls, Hoffman was confined to the Otter Tail County jail. After the necessary paperwork and legal procedures were followed, Knutson was on his way back to his office when he was accosted by Nils Anderson, of the firm of Anderson, Anderson, and Balik. "I understand you have arrested one of my clients. I'd like to talk to him, if I may?"

"Now, who would that be?"

"David Hoffman."

"Since when?"

"Since about five minutes after you arrested him, apparently. His wife called and insisted that I represent him. To be perfectly frank, I don't even remember meeting the man, but his wife says that I did some kind of legal work for them in connection with a deed a few years ago. I told her that I'd never handled a murder case before, but she insisted I get down here and represent her husband. Can I see him for a few minutes?"

"Yah, I guess so. I'll take you in and, well, I guess I'll reintroduce you. Follow me."

Knutson arranged a secure room for the lawyer and his client. After a surprisingly short time, the lawyer emerged and said, "Sheriff, my client says he would like to talk to you. I've advised him that he should not speak until I have had a chance to study his case, but he is adamant that he should see you."

"Very well, although I would also like another officer present, and I would like to tape the conversation. Is that acceptable?"

"In fact, I told him that you would no doubt want to do that. Again, against my recommendations, he wants to go on record at this time."

Palmer shrugged and said, "It's fine with me. Give me a few minutes to get the recording equipment ready and let me find my deputy. Meanwhile, why don't you get back to your client? I suspect that we are about to hear a confession of murder."

The sheriff found Orly just as he was putting on his coat. "Going somewhere?"

The deputy, who had been thinking about sneaking out a little early so he could drive up to Moorhead and visit his girlfriend Allysha, hesitated. "Er, well, this seems to be sort of wrapped up and I thought maybe, well, I've got a couple of things to do yet today and so I thought I'd, you know, get started on them."

"Yah, sure. Well, never mind. Hoffman's already got a lawyer and it seems he's ready to spill it all. I thought you'd want to be there."

Under most circumstances, Orly would rather have been with Allysha, but this was different. "Yes, I do. Let's go."

Orly followed the sheriff to a small, windowless room. In the center of the room was a small, rectangular table with four chairs. Orly and Palmer sat on one side of the table facing Nils Anderson and his client. No one spoke as Knutson methodically plugged in the small tape recorder and tested it. Satisfied, Knutson spoke into the microphone.

"The date is February third, 2006. The place is an interview room in the Otter Tail County Law Enforcement Center, Fergus Falls, Minnesota. The suspect is David Hoffman, known previously as David Hart. He is represented at this interview by his counsel, Nils Anderson. Also present is Orly Peterson, Deputy Sheriff of Otter Tail County, and me, Palmer Knutson, Sheriff of Otter Tail County. The suspect has been apprised of his rights, has given us permission to record this interview, and is cooperating under his own will."

Orly looked over at David Hart, a.k.a. David Hoffman. Although he had been, at one time, the subject of one of the largest FBI manhunts in American history, he looked even smaller than he had back at the Otter Slide. He had not yet been made to put on his orange prison jumpsuit, and still wore his off-brand denim jeans and a rather new plaid flannel shirt. As Orly looked down, he half expected to see bear slippers on his feet. This was the guy that J. Edgar Hoover had once claimed was more dangerous than Dillinger?

"State your full name, please," said the sheriff mechanically.

"My real name is David Glen Hart. I was born April 2, 1947, in Galesburg, Illinois. For the last thirty-four years I have been living under the name of David Hoffman."

"Mr. Hart, will you tell us the circumstances that led you to change your name?"

"I can't tell you how glad I am to hear somebody call me by my real name again. In some ways, that has been the hardest thing over this last quarter century—to completely cut myself off from all that I had lived before. I cried when I learned that my father had died, not only because he died not knowing where I was, but also because I was not there to comfort my mother. I don't know what happened to my sisters. They are probably married with children. If so, those kids have a fugitive uncle they have never seen and I would guess my sisters would be too ashamed to tell them about me. But most of all, it's the little things—you know, to read about somebody else named Hart in the paper and think, 'I used to be a Hart.' There were many times when I would have given myself up had it not been for my wife's ability to give me courage. She has always been there for me."

Hart paused, and smiled as he examined a corner of the ceiling, apparently reflecting on the devotion of his wife. Knutson did not hurry him, and after a while, he continued. "You see, I was always kind of a loner, an unpopular kid in high school. I was a good enough student, but I never, well, nobody ever cared about that. When I got to college, it was the same thing. I'd do well in class, but none of my professors ever remembered who I was. Like everybody else, I let my hair grow long and grew a full beard, rather scraggly, I guess. I've relived those days often, over the last few years, and I've come to the conclusion that I got into radical politics more to belong to something than because I passionately believed in it. I mean, sure, we all believed in civil rights and the protection of the underprivileged. I still do. And incidentally, Sheriff, I've read about your wife's political activities and I admire her greatly. Please tell her that. But looking back, just remember the times! The United States had no business being in Vietnam, it was immoral and wrong. The draft policies were racist and the military-industrial machine cranked out obscene profits on the bones of innocent people on both sides. I still believe that. But like I said, in Iowa City in 1970, everybody believed it, but not everybody blew up buildings and killed a librarian. In fact, I had no intention of doing things like that when I first got involved in our group. We didn't even have a name, you know, like 'The Weathermen' in Wisconsin—and although the press called us a 'Weathermen faction' we didn't communicate with anyone else as far as I know. Anyway, when I got involved I just felt accepted like I had never been before. Accepted for who I was. But most of all, I suppose I kept it up because of Sharon. No girl had ever really paid any attention to me before, and Sharon, she was nice to me from the start.

"Well, I'm not going to bore you with that, but it really is part of the story. You see, everyone said what we needed to do was to create an event—not a simple sign-carrying march or a brick through the window of Iowa Book and Stationery (or Iowa Book and Crook, as we called it), but a real big 'Take that, Nixon!' event. Somebody came up with the idea that we could paralyze the university if we took out the library. Now, there were a lot of intellectuals in our movement, and the idea of destroying books was more than many of us could take. So somebody else suggested that we just render it temporarily unusable. This one guy was a graduate student in chemistry, and he said he could make a smoke-and-stink bomb that would spread throughout the building, would not destroy the books, but would leave it unusable for a month. It would be a nice, nonviolent protest. There were a few who thought it was a wimp-out—they still wanted a real bomb—but the rest of us thought it was a great plan.

"At this point in our relationship, I thought Sharon was starting to lose interest in me and when talk got started as to who would place the bomb, I got sort of carried away and volunteered. That night, the group met me near the library and handed me this cheap, locked, plastic briefcase. I walked in, put it where they had told me to, and ran out. I'd never been so scared in my life. I panicked and ran, and as I looked back over my shoulder I suddenly crashed into a man and we both fell down in a heap. Suddenly we both heard this tremendous explosion. I was totally confused. 'Surely,' I thought, 'all that noise cannot have come from a smoke bomb.' I looked back and saw flames and I heard people scream and I knew that I had been played for a sucker. I had never, ever, ever meant to hurt anybody. That moment is still frozen in time for me, because I looked into this man's eyes and he looked into mine and I just felt that he had somehow sensed my desperation. I could never forget those eyes, because they seemed accusatory and compassionate at the same time. More than likely they were just the look of a surprised man who has been run into. In any event, I never saw those eyes again until last Friday night, when John Hofstead walked into our resort.

"Well, after I ran away from the library, I went back to my apartment, and Sharon was already there. She helped me throw a few things into my attaché case." Hart smiled, "I know, you're thinking, 'a hippy with an attaché case?' Yeah, I got it from my folks when I went off to college. It even had a nice set of initials on either side of the handle—'D. H.' Sharon, meanwhile, had gone out and got a car. She 'arranged' to steal it. That is, a friend gave us the car and told us to go anywhere we wanted to and leave it near a police station and he would report it stolen after three days. We got in and drove and drove and drove until we got to New Mexico. We were so tired we finally checked into a motel. The desk clerk asked us our name, looking down at my fancy attaché case with my initials on it. I suppose no one has ever praised me for my quick wit, and *The Graduate* had come out not too long before and that was hot stuff. I told them my name was David Hoffman and even grinned and said, 'No relation to Dustin.'"

The confessed murderer took a deep breath and made a winsome smile. "So that started it, our life on the run. The next day we bought a newspaper and there was a big story on the bombing and on the tragic death of that woman. I felt horrible—I wanted to give myself up there and then. But Sharon, well, Sharon said that no one would believe that I didn't do it on purpose and that I wasn't really a murderer after all. I believed her because I wanted to believe her, I guess.

"I shaved my beard and cut my hair and got a pair of black plastic glasses to replace my wire rims. We stopped at a used clothing store and got some gabardine slacks and a few shirts and ties. Sharon got a few dresses. Actually, it was sort of a hoot at the time. We played like we were young Republicans and called each other David Eisenhower and Julie Nixon. We stayed down there, avoiding anything like a countercultureal environment, and eventually we got jobs, put money in the bank, and saved enough money to come here and build the Otter Slide. In fact we are both quite proud of what we have done with the place.

"But that was David Hoffman. I know, no matter how many times I have tried to forget it, that David Hart killed a person. If I don't remember it, my dreams do. When I saw Mr. Hofstead, I knew that he recognized me. I knew it would be only a matter of time before he told somebody about it. I suppose he told his wife before he died."

At this point, Knutson broke into the long narrative with a simple, "So that's why you killed him?"

"Killed Hofstead?" Hart squinted and looked confused. "He died in an accident!"

The deputy stood up violently, and leaned over to glare into Hart's eyes. "I know that's how you tried to make it look, but give it up! There was no way that the snowmobile could have traveled from the statue to the lake after Hofstead fell off of it without somebody else driving it there. Your fingerprints are all over the sled and all over the helmet that Hofstead was wearing. We assume that you whacked Hofstead on the head, dumped him out by the loon, and left him to freeze to death. We will be searching the Otter Slide for a murder weapon, and I'm sure we'll find it. You've already confessed to causing the death of a poor woman in Iowa City—why don't you save us all time and confess to killing Hofstead as well? We already have enough evidence for a conviction. By sticking to that ridiculous accident story you are just going to mortgage the Otter Slide in legal costs, and then where will your wife be? Just get it off your chest."

Hart looked away for a long time. Finally he turned to Nils Anderson, who had no stomach for a murder trial in the first place, especially one that he was certain to lose. Anderson seemed to raise his eyebrows as if to say, "Well? Can we get it over with?" Still Hart did not speak. He ran his fingers over his graying and balding scalp and Orly noticed, with some embarrassment, that he was crying.

At last he said, "I did it. I hit him with a hammer in the shed, put him in his suit, and dumped him at the loon. Then I walked back. Can I go back to my cell now?"

TWENTY-FOUR

"MR. SPORTS, MR. ACTION, Mr. Jim Ed Poole," were the first words Palmer Knutson heard through the darkness of a new day. For a time, he stared at the radio clock, unable to comprehend that it was really 6:40 in the morning. He had slept badly. Ellie, bless her heart, had decided that a successful end to a murder investigation deserved something special. She had made Palmer's favorite, beef Stroganov, and served it with a rather expensive Cabernet Sauvignon. Reluctantly, Palmer thought to himself, "I've got to get another favorite meal. This one is killing me." He hadn't kept count, but the food must have consumed forty-seven times its weight in Rolaids. He loved red wine, but it always gave him a headache. He had tossed and turned all night, and now his tongue felt like it was coated in creosote.

When he had slept, he had dreamed. The dreams made no sense, but were a jumble of high school memories and events peopled with individuals from the recent past. He thought he would tell Ellie about them, but when he opened his mouth to do so, he realized he remembered nothing. He reached over and lovingly patted his wife to see if she was awake. Ellie was proud of herself for serving Palmer's favorite meal, as well she should have been, for she was an excellent cook, but as she turned on the light and gave him a pleasant morning smile, he wondered if he dared to suggest that next time they celebrated it should be with a nice chicken salad.

The sheriff was reluctant to get out of bed, but he knew it would be a busy day. There was paperwork to suffer through, calls to make, and he had to meet with the media who always found murder so fascinating. At last he heard Trygve get up and decided he could put it off no longer. He went down to make coffee while Ellie helped Trygve get his own breakfast. This endeavor required much more work than if Ellie had just done it herself, but she consoled herself that, in the long run, she was preparing him for life.

Palmer took his coffee over to the kitchen table and quietly stared off into space. He administered the usual "you better hurry or you're going to be late" advice to Trygve, but his heart just wasn't in it. When their son had finally gone off to school, Ellie refilled his cup and sat down across from him. "What's the matter?" she asked gently.

"Huh, oh, nothing, nothing. I just didn't get much sleep last night, that's all."

"Are you feeling all right?"

"Sure, it's just that, oh, I don't know what it is. Something keeps gnawing at me about the Hofstead case."

Ellie scowled, "But you have the evidence and you have a confession. What more could you want?"

Palmer sucked the cooler coffee off the surface of the cup in an unattractive slurp and agreed. "Right. It's cut and dried from here on out. But it's funny, you know. We had this core group of people who knew the victim, a man who was going to cause a big change in their lives, and it wasn't one of them that killed him. Instead, it was some guy he had the bad luck to meet again after over thirty years. It's just so coincidental. Like I told Orly, it's a fluke."

"Well that may be, dear, but remember that Hofstead would probably have caused a big change in Hoffman's life, or Hart's if you prefer, if he had lived. What's the difference?"

"Promise you won't bring it up again if I tell you? Orly's already enjoying the fact that I said it."

"All right, I promise. What is it?"

"The guy doesn't seem like a murderer." After a pause, he repeated himself, "He just doesn't seem like one!"

"So what's wrong with feeling that way?"

"Don't you see? It runs counter to the facts. I would have been totally blind to David Hoffman ever being a killer unless the fluke with the fingerprint happened."

Ellie shrugged and dismissed his concerns. "So you can't be right all of the time." Ellie paused and stared at her husband over the rim of her coffee cup. "But you know what I think, Palmer? I think that after all these years of being sheriff, your feelings are sometimes more accurate than somebody else's facts. So they weren't in this case. So what? 'Trust the Force, Luke.'"

"Thanks, Ellie. I suppose I'd better get going."

But the sheriff didn't go. Instead, he sat staring at the wallpaper while he held a piece of toast halfway to his mouth. Ellie knew better than to bother him at times like this, and she tried to interest herself in an old *Newsweek*. At last, Palmer shoved the cold toast in his mouth and said, "I think I'm going to take a little time this morning and go home. I haven't been there in the winter for a long time."

Ellie, who knew what "home" meant to her husband, smiled knowingly and said, "Want another cup of coffee before you go?"

Before he left the house, Palmer called his deputy. "Orly? Look, I'm going to be a little late this morning. There are a couple of things I need to think through ... Huh? Yah, matter of fact, I am going up to the home place ... No, nothing's wrong with the case, at least part of it, anyway. There are just a few loose ends I want to clear up, that's all. But I should be back before noon. Try to keep the media happy ... Sure, you're welcome to that duty. Tell them everything you think they need to know ... You mean, our investigations surrounding Hofstead Hail? Probably not, at least for the moment. I mean, there's this meeting this morning and everybody is sure to be in a little state of shock when they see how it turns out. There will be a pretty significant absence at the meeting! ... What? You figure it out!"

The sheriff drove his Acura to a lonely place about four miles outside of the village of Underwood. The county snowplow had passed and left a wide shoulder on the gravel road. Knutson sat in the warm car and read again the report from the Bureau of Criminal Apprehension. It was short on detail, but long on significance. The three sets of prints found on the snowmobile, the helmet, and the zipper pull were all traced to Hofstead, Sharon Hoffman, and the man who called himself David Hoffman. No other prints were found anywhere. David Hart's prints were found in several places on both the helmet and the snowmobile, and it was a simple matter to run them through the computer until they hit the jackpot. Since Mrs. Hoffman assisted her husband in the resort business, it was only to be expected that her prints would also be there. Still, as Palmer pulled down the fur flaps of his hat over his ears and prepared to inspect his old home, the seeming incongruity of David Hoffman being a murderer nagged at him.

"Home" was now little more than a two-acre patch of ground connected to the road by a dirt approach. Once, it had been a farmstead, built by Palmer's grandfather shortly after he came over from Norway in the 1890s. The original small house had grown as the Knutson family increased, and in time a large red barn, a chicken coop, a granary, a hog shed, and an outhouse had graced the property. This was the only home Palmer had known until he went off to the army. It was the home of a weeping willow, of a tire swing, of kittens in the barn, of morning glories climbing up the windmill, of little wooden boats that Palmer made and sailed, sharing the stock tank with the noses of thirty head of cattle. It was the home of a little boy who spoke a lot more Norwegian than English when he had started first grade, and Palmer sometimes felt like he needed to get in touch with that little boy again.

There were two pieces of evidence that this had once been a farmstead. The first was a thin line of box elders that ran to the north and west of where the buildings had stood. The second was a tall windmill, standing stark against the cloudy gray sky. Its wind blades were still largely intact, and, as the cold wind blew, the wheel turned with an eerie creaking voice as if it were a fifty-foot skeleton standing watch over an abandoned graveyard. Palmer stepped out of his car and waded in the snow toward where the house used to be. The wind changed direction and the windmill screamed as if to warn him to turn back.

Palmer stood where, as a boy, he had built one of his best snow forts. The wind had created a drift that ran between the house and the weeping willow tree. The drift became so hard that he could climb the side and leap from the top and catch the tire swing and sway like Tarzan before he jumped into a soft pile of snow. On the other side of the drift, he had carved an entrance into his private cave. He remembered how he had been able to stand up straight in his little cavern and mentally projected the drift to have been about seven feet high. Then, as a smile crept across his face, he realized that for him to have been able to stand up straight when he was nine years old would have required a much smaller snowdrift. He looked down into the pit that had been the basement of his house. The current owner of the farm was using it as a place to dump rocks. "No," he said to himself, "it would be hard to play with my wind-up train set down there this winter." He wandered around thinking about families and husbands and wives and how his parents had struggled on the farm, and how Mr. and Mrs. Hofstead had lived together for so long, and how Gary and Faye Janice seemed to embody what couples were like today, and how David and Sharon had shared a life on the run for more than thirty years. To what extent would couples go to help each other? He turned to look where the old barn had been and suddenly the wind shifted and blew a wisp of snow right into his neck. He automatically reached down and pulled the zipper up under his chin. It was like the cruel wind blew an idea into his head. He didn't like the idea, but as he took a last look around home, he knew it was right. There were telephone calls to make, more paperwork, and another arrest warrant to be made out, but now, at last, the whole truth would be told.

TWENTY-FIVE

LATER THAT MORNING, PALMER Knutson sat at his desk, staring blankly at his framed map of Norway. He wondered at what point devotion ended and dependency began. How could one spouse be so dependent on the other as to mortgage their collective future? Or maybe it was just old-fashioned gallantry? Would he do it for Ellie? Would Ellie do it for him? Perhaps it was unfortunate that the law had to step in and preclude a noble act from interfering with justice. But in this kind of inner argument, the sheriff inevitably came back to a logical formula, "if justice is perverted, can the act be considered noble?" In this case, Knutson decided it could not. It was in the midst of this brown study that Orly Peterson knocked and, as was his annoying habit, entered at the same time.

"Palmer, I need to talk to you. I've been thinking about the Hofstead murder."

The sheriff sipped his coffee, sighed, and set down his cup. "Yah, Orly, so have I. Sit down. No, wait. Go get yourself a cup of coffee. In fact, get me one. There are a few things I've been waiting to tell you."

Orly returned shortly with two cups of coffee and sat across from the sheriff.

"Now, then. What's on your mind?"

"It's Hoffman, or Hart—whatever his name is," blurted the deputy. "I don't think he killed Hofstead."

"All right. But he's confessed to it. What makes you say he didn't do it?"

"Actually, it was something you said this morning. Although you assured me that there was nothing the matter with the case— how could there be, with a confession?—I got the feeling that you were dissatisfied with the outcome. Then you said that when I met with the media I should avoid going into the whole Hofstead Hail scenario. Finally, you said that there would be one significant absence when the meeting took place. So I began to think, what if Hart, although without a doubt the man wanted in the bombing at the University of Iowa, is not the killer of Hofstead? How could it be anybody else?"

"And?"

"Hart is lying. You saw how surprised he was when we even brought up the fact that we were arresting him for Hofstead's murder. He expected to be arrested for the bombing, but he acted as though he had never even thought that Hofstead's death was anything but an accident. Added to this, of course, was the demeanor of the man himself. Now I know we have talked about never judging by appearances, *et cetera, et cetera*. But, you can't deny that hunches or feelings are important, and I've never had the feeling that he could have killed anybody. At least intentionally, of course.

So why would he say he did? Simple. Because he thinks his wife did it. You heard from the testimony how Sharon had saved his bacon in Iowa City? Now he thinks she killed Hofstead, and taking the rap for her would be the least he could do."

"Why would he assume his wife did it?" Knutson asked, noncommittally.

"Don't you see? That's the other half of the romantic, *A Tale of Two Cities* kind of sacrifice. He thinks that she thinks he is going to be identified by Hofstead. He assumes that she would protect him now like she did all those years ago. He thinks he can't let her make that kind of sacrifice again."

"And you're saying she didn't make that kind of sacrifice?"

"Of course she didn't. The motive was not nearly so romantic. The motive for Hofstead's murder was common greed and ambition."

"Go on," the sheriff said patiently, "whose common greed and ambition?"

"As I said," Orly began, becoming more animated as he began to explain his deductions, "it was you who got me thinking about the people involved in Hofstead Hail once again. Now, I asked myself, who of that group would have the most to gain by Hofstead's death?

"Myron Pekanen? Not likely. Nobody really expected him be the new president, not even, apparently, himself. If he had a motive, it would have had to involve something we don't know now, like maybe a financial fiddle that Hofstead had just discovered. And there has really never been any suggestion that Pekanen is anything other than an honest and efficient insurance man. To be sure, I thought for a time that there might be some Iowa City connection with Pekanen, since he was there at the same time Hofstead was, but supposedly they didn't even know each other then and there is really no reason to doubt this.

"His wife," Peterson methodically continued, "also could have done it. And there we get into the romantic angle again. Would she kill for her husband? Probably not. Would she kill for the chance to boost their financial and social standing? She might. In fact, I think she would be more likely to do it than her husband. Not that I think her husband is above killing anybody, but I think he's the kind to get into a knife fight when he's drunk and end up killing somebody. But premeditated murder? I can't see it.

"Then there's the Sandbergs. Neither of them would hurt a fly. Besides, everyone sort of assumed that Clarence would get the job. Why would killing Hofstead benefit either of them? I suppose there could be a situation where a change might reveal some financial irregularities, but if there were any on Sandberg's part, you can be sure they were screw-ups instead of any venal scheme. His wife? That nice old Joey? Don't be silly! So I crossed off the Sandbergs."

Knutson listened to his lengthy monologue, quietly sipping his coffee and nodding his agreement in several, but not all, places. Peterson, gratified by Knutson's complete attention and approving expression, continued. "So that brings us to Borghild and Harry Kvamme. Now that could be kind of interesting. We established that both had snowmobile experience and that, in fact, neither could even provide an alibi for the other. Suppose Borghild thinks, 'After all these years of devoted service to this guy, he's going to turn around and give the job of president to somebody else, passing me over like I didn't exist.' Remember, she says, and Mrs. Hofstead supports her on this, that she had no idea he was going to

221

pick her. If she assumed he'd pick Sandberg or Swenson, well, it could have been the straw that broke the camel's back.

"Harry, now that's an interesting suggestion. He doesn't seem involved in the company much at all. But he's a strong and independent man. Suppose Hofstead meets with him and suggests that he is going to make his wife the new president of the company. Maybe Harry thinks he wants his wife to be just dear little Borghild, not climbing above her station. So he gets in a fight, which I can envision him doing, and he slugs Hofstead. Hofstead goes down, Harry panics, and dumps him by the loon. I know, this is not likely, but it is an interesting thought.

"Martha Hofstead herself? If she did it, she is a terrific actress. So maybe, I tell myself, she is a terrific actress. After all, she gets everything. Suppose she is finally fed up with living in Fergus Falls with this nice but predictable husband and all she has to look forward to is her retirement years with this nice but predictable husband. On the surface, after all, who benefits more than anyone else by Hofstead's death? The now-wealthy widow. She's still a good-looking woman, and with plenty of money she could have a grand old time for another twenty years. Nobody can support her claim that she spent the whole time in her room. She knew how to operate a snowmobile. For all we know, she could have hit him over the head with the telephone in their room, stuffed him in his snowmobile suit, and staged the loon attack. But I don't think she did."

"No," said the sheriff, "I'm certain she did not. Go on."

"Okay. So I also dismiss the insurance angle. This Laura Epperly life insurance policy was just sort of an unusual side angle. She has never even been to Fergus Falls. Neither the Fergus Falls State University Scholarship fund nor Concordia College are likely to need money so badly that they will murder for it. So who's left? I'll tell you who. A couple of the coolest killers you're ever going to find, Gary Swenson and Faye Janice Nelson!"

If Orly was expecting the sheriff to jump up and shout in shock and astonishment, he was disappointed. Knutson's expression remained as unchanged as the Mona Lisa's. He merely said, "How did you arrive at that conclusion?"

"As usual, the combination of means, motive, and opportunity. First the motive. Swenson sees himself as the rising star. He sells more insurance than anyone else, he modernizes the whole operation. Hofstead is going to retire, and Swenson thinks he has earned the job. But, he thinks that Hofstead is going with his old crony Sandberg. Swenson detests Sandberg, and thinks the old rise to the top will come to an abrupt end. He has spent the last few years schmoozing around Martha Hofstead and assumes he has won her over with his charm. John Hofstead might pick Clarence, he figures, but Martha will not pick Clarence and will pick him instead. Simple as that. But he has help. Notice how they are really into the couple thing. Faye Janice and Gary do everything together, including murder. Faye Janice likes the finer things in life. She likes material possessions. She likes the idea of skiing in Vail and surfing in Hawaii. You saw her office at the university—she is hardly into the academics of physical education, if such a thing really does exist. So she is ready to help her ambitious husband.

"Now, means and opportunity are the best for them. Who are the last out on the lake? Gary, Faye Janice, and Hofstead. One of them distracts the victim while the other hits him with a wrench they had brought along for the purpose. Gary loads Hofstead back on his own snowmobile and takes him over to the loon. Faye Janice follows him on her sled. Gary stages the accident, drives the snowmobile to the clear ice, and Faye Janice gives him a ride back to his own sled. They go back to the Otter Slide. Pekanen is still out drinking, and this confuses the whole issue of who is back and who is not. The Swensons, of course, or the Swenson-Nelsons or whatever you want to call them, have each other to provide alibis. The next day they can act as shocked as everybody else. Do we have proof of this? No, unfortunately we don't. But, I would bet that if we had them in and separately interrogated them they would crack like a gallon of two-dollar paint."

Knutson smiled sardonically and said, "You'd lose."

"Huh?" Orly looked up anxiously. "What do you mean?"

"I mean, you'd lose your bet. They wouldn't crack, because they had nothing to do with it. By the way, before I say anything more, I want to apologize for my statement this morning that there would be a significant absence at the Hofstead Hail meeting this morning. I didn't mean the killer would not be there. I was just thinking of John Hofstead, and what a good man he was, and I just meant that he wouldn't be there. Sorry if I misled you."

"Yah, well, if Gary and Faye Janice didn't kill him, it was Hart after all, huh?"

"I didn't say that. In fact, much of what you surmised was right on. There is a bit of *A Tale of Two Cities* romanticism here. I had never thought of it that way, but it's not bad, somebody giving up his life for another. And, I guess, it's not only been on one side, although the romance seems to be more on one side than the other.

"You see, Hart never really meant to kill anyone. Earlier this morning I was walking around where our old house had been. The wind started blowing snow down my neck and I pulled the zipper up to my chin. Ellie, as a joke, put this silly Uncle Scrooge Mc-Duck thing she got out of a cereal box on my zipper pull and I've never gotten around to taking it off. Anyway, it reminded me of something I had read in the BCA report, or rather, I should say, it reminded me of something I didn't read there. According to the report, only three sets of prints were found—Hofstead's, David Hoffman's, and Sharon Hoffman's. It said that David Hoffman's prints were found on the helmet and on the snowmobile. Earlier, it had been ascertained that there were two sets of prints on the zipper-pull. In other words, there was a second set of prints on the zipper-pull made by the person who had zipped Hofstead into the snowmobile suit. And that person was not, according to the report, David Hoffman.

"So, therefore … yah, that's right, it was Sharon Hoffman. Sharon Hoffman, who has one of the most selective consciences I have ever run across. I decided to go right out to the Otter Slide and take her in for questioning. When I got there, I discovered that she had packed up and left, leaving behind this extremely brief note for me. Let me share this with you."

Dear Sheriff:

I realize that it will only be a matter of time before you are out here again. By the time you read this, I will be on the road one more time. You will not be able to find me because I have grown quite adept at assuming another life. I do want to make one thing clear, however, and that is that my husband David was guiltless in the bombing of the University of Iowa library and in the death of that librarian. It was I who removed the harmless bomb and substituted one that, unfortunately, killed a person. I regret that this person had to die, but her death at least contributed to the outrage of the people, and the outrage of the people helped end the murder in Vietnam. In the end, actions such as ours saved thousands of lives on both sides. I apologize not for the act, but for the fact that David has carried the burden of guilt around with him for all these years. Please give my husband this message: 'I'll never forget you, David. We helped change the world.'

"—and it's signed Sharon Kline; presumably that was her original name."

"Huh!" grunted Orly, "but nowhere in that letter does she …"

"Exactly," Knutson said, "Nowhere does she even mention John Hofstead. This is what I meant when I said she has a selective conscience. But she killed him, and I can prove it. What I find interesting is that in 1970 she was willing to dupe Hart into thinking he was putting down a stink bomb in the library when the pathetic loser was really carrying a lethal package. Then she let him suffer for all those years. Why? I guess, in her way, she loved him—at least, she liked the fact that here was a person who was totally dependent on her. It will be interesting to see what kind of background we can find on this Sharon Kline. Anyway, for all this time they have been living this masquerade, with David adoring Sharon for the way she had protected him, never suspecting that she was, in truth, the real murderer of that librarian. Now, when Hofstead comes out to the Otter Slide and spots Hart, it looks like her husband will be exposed. Of course, if he is, so is she. She decides to kill Hofstead, and she does it pretty much as we have surmised.

Meanwhile, her husband thinks it is just a very unfortunate accident, and his only worry is whether or not Hofstead spilled the beans about his identity before he died.

"Now, yesterday, when we told him we were arresting him for the murder of Hofstead, I noticed the same thing you did, that is, total bewilderment on his part that a murder had been committed at all, much less by him. But he quickly put two and two together and decided if it were not him, it was his wife. He decided that if she was willing to kill for him, he was willing to go to prison for her."

"What's going to happen to the poor sap?"

"Well," the sheriff began, thoughtfully. "That's not really for us to say, is it? But I would guess they will probably reduce that Iowa charge to manslaughter. I'm sure he'll serve a little time. He really is quite a silly and pathetic person, but you can't help sort of admiring him. I can't help but wonder—"

The telephone interrupted Knutson's line of thought. "Yah, put him through. Yah, this is Palmer Knutson ... Yah, I thought you might! ... Oh really? ... Oh really? ... Huh! Yah, I wouldn't doubt it ... Oh, I don't know. I just thought that she would be the type to avoid an obvious place like the Minneapolis airport. Her car was gone and I thought, 'Who knows, she might still have some old connections there.' We did chase a lot of them up there then, you know ... Yah, sure. Thanks."

"That was the United States border patrol at Pembina, North Dakota. It seems that a woman matching the description of Sharon Hoffman—or Kline, or whatever she's calling herself—passed through customs late yesterday afternoon. The border guard remembers her because, when he asked her the purpose of her visit to Canada, she had blandly replied that she was just there for a couple days of shopping. The guard tried to be friendly and suggested that they had some good deals on fur coats at The Bay. He was called a Nazi and treated to a lecture on animal rights. Oh, yah, he couldn't forget her."

"You know," the sheriff continued, "they say the Mounties always get their man. I'm not so sure they will be able to get this woman. In any event, somebody needs to go up to Manitoba with the details…"

Orly saw his plans for the weekend, which centered around the lovely Allysha, take wings and fly toward the window. His face had the expression of a kid who'd eagerly bit into what looked like a chocolate chip cookie, only to find raisins.

"…so I was thinking this would best be handled if you drove your own car up to Winnipeg and the county would pay your mileage. And since it is your car, and since you will be passing through Moorhead anyway, perhaps you'd like a passenger. There are a lot of fun things to do in Winnipeg on a weekend, even in winter. Or perhaps Allysha would be too busy? You would have a chance to liaise with the Royal Canadian Mounted Police. Who knows, maybe you could even get a Mountie hat!"

Orly knew that the sheriff was ribbing him, yet, he could not help but imagine how great he would look in an RCMP hat, and maybe he and Allysha could do a little shopping at the Hudson Bay store, and the county should be able to pay at least part of the hotel bill… Why not stay at the Fort Garry and then they could…

At that moment, Borghild Kvamme was concluding her speech to the employees of Hofstead Hail. "One more thing. I will continue to make coffee around here, if I find the pot empty and the need is there. I expect the rest of you to do the same. If you take the last cup, then you make the next pot. I'm not even sure if all of you know how to make coffee, but if you're going to drink it from now on, you'd better learn. I will continue to bring cookies, sometimes, but you'd better take your turn as well. The same goes for cleaning up after yourself. I intend to hire a secretary, and quite soon, but she, or he, will do her work and take her turn with the coffee like everybody else. Now, it is noontime and I suppose you will want your lunch. But I've always felt a good time to approach farmers about hail insurance is when they're not so busy. Like in February!

"So after lunch, get out there and sell some insurance!"

THE END

ABOUT THE AUTHOR

Gerald Anderson is a former history professor at North Dakota State University, where he taught Modern European and British history for twenty-one years, and in 2005 received the Robert Odney Excellence in Education Award from NDSU. He has studied extensively in Europe, and holds an MA from NDSU and a PhD from the University of Iowa (1973).

He is the author of *Fascists, Communists, and the National Government*, a two-volume *Study Guide for the Western Perspective*, and articles and reviews concerning British, European, and Scandinavian-American history in various periodicals. In addition to works in his academic field, Anderson published his first novel, *The Uffda Trial*, in 1994. He is a native of Hitterdal, Minnesota.